A VILLAGE MURDER

A HAM HILL MURDER MYSTERY

FRANCES EVESHAM

Boldwood

First published in Great Britain in 2020 by Boldwood Books Ltd.

Copyright © Frances Evesham, 2020

Cover Design by Nick Castle Design

A CIP catalogue record for this book is available from the British Library.

Paperback ISBN 978-1-80048-064-3

Large Print ISBN 978-1-80048-063-6

Ebook ISBN 978-1-80048-066-7

Kindle ISBN 978-1-80048-065-0

Audio CD ISBN 978-1-80048-058-2

MP3 CD ISBN 978-1-80048-059-9

Digital audio download ISBN 978-1-80048-060-5

Boldwood Books Ltd
23 Bowerdean Street
London SW6 3TN
www.boldwoodbooks.com

1

THE PLOUGH

Adam Hennessy rose early; he had beer taps to polish, a bar to wipe clean and optics to fill. He yawned. He needed to find another barman, fast. The Plough had heaved with thirsty locals last night, and he'd been run off his feet.

He leaned on a windowsill, as he did every morning, to view Ham Hill above the village, still visible through pouring April rain cascading down the uneven glass of the sixteenth century window.

He yawned again. Sleep. That's what he needed. He'd be at The Streamside Hotel all afternoon, for Councillor Jones' wake; Lower Hembrow's biggest social event this year. Pity he would be there to serve, not on the guest list.

Still, if you can't do a favour for your neighbours, don't live in an English village.

Was there time for a nap before lunch?

He walked through to the private rooms at one end of the long, low building. An easel leaned against the wall of the sitting room, inviting Adam to pick up a brush, but the desire for sleep trumped everything, just now.

A muffled thump shook the back door. What was that?

'Come in,' Adam called, heart sinking at the interruption. 'It's not locked.'

No one entered, so he cracked the door open an inch. Ex-detectives know better than to casually throw their doors wide at every knock.

With an ear-splitting crunch, the safety chain zinged from the door frame and a whirlwind of fur punched Adam in the chest.

He staggered back, grabbing the door for support. The guided missile, a shaggy brown dog, thudded two muddy paws on his shoulders and washed his face with sticky dribble.

'Get down,' Adam spluttered. 'You've broken my door.'

The dog, representing no recognisable breed, took a step back, head on one side, watching Adam's every move from a pair of huge brown eyes. Apparently satisfied, it slurped water from a puddle on the path.

It was thin, just skin and bone, and wore no collar.

'Where did you come from?'

The dog came closer, water dripping from its muzzle.

Adam hesitated. He didn't understand dogs. Cats, he liked, but dogs made him nervous.

He waved an arm towards the garden gate, hoping the dog would leave as suddenly as it had arrived.

Instead, it settled on its haunches, one paw in the air.

So much for that nap.

'I suppose you're hungry.' Adam strode through the sitting room into the bar, the dog at his heels. 'You can't come in the kitchen, though, I'll lose my licence.'

He shooed the creature back, kicked the kitchen door shut and pulled a can of corned beef from a shelf. Why on earth had The Plough's chef ordered it? Adam hated corned beef; had done since childhood. His mother hadn't been much of a cook.

He emptied the beef into an old dish and took it outside to his little courtyard garden. The dog, feathery tail swishing, whimpered with delight, buried its head deep in the bowl and hoovered up every scrap of food, as though perfectly at home in The Plough.

Adam rubbed his chin. Where could this creature have come from, and why had he chosen The Plough for his new home?

* * *

Imogen Bishop floored the accelerator. Her long-suffering Land Rover, gardening equipment clanking in the back, sped through Lower Hembrow. On two wheels, it squealed through the entrance to The Streamside Hotel, narrowly missing one of the Georgian pillars.

Late for her own father's funeral? What kind of daughter was she?

She winced and slowed a fraction, racketing past the hotel's half-filled car park.

The Land Rover screeched to a halt at the back of the building. Imogen hauled herself from the driver's seat, slammed the door, checked her watch for the twentieth time and made a dash for the entrance, calculating. She had just enough time for a quick shower.

What had possessed her to spend the entire morning pricking out lettuces and tomatoes? Designing the gardens at Haselbury House was her biggest, most prestigious project ever, but she had no need to be there every day. That was the project manager's job.

It was too wet for outdoor work today, anyway. Planting potatoes would have to wait for another day, when her father's funeral was over, the weather had cleared, and Imogen's head was no longer spinning.

She leapt up the back stairs, taking them two at a time. She'd been procrastinating all morning, dreading the thought of her father's burial next to her beloved mother, and she'd almost left it too late.

She looked away as she passed the door to her father's bedroom. He'd owned The Streamside Hotel since Imogen was eleven, living in these rooms the whole time, although she'd moved away from the village as soon as she'd left school.

Before long, she'd have to pluck up the courage to sort his books, collect his reading glasses from the bedside drawer and send his clothes to charity. Those were jobs for another day, when she felt stronger. She'd been in limbo, in a state of shock, ever since that day two weeks ago when the police arrived at her flat with the news of her father's sudden death.

The coroner had blamed slippery roads, fly-tipped rubbish and thinning tyres for the accident. One of her father's oldest friends, he'd made only a brief reference to the level of alcohol in the councillor's bloodstream.

Imogen pushed the thought away. No time for that now. She hadn't seen eye-to-eye with her father for years, but there was no excuse for arriving late at his funeral.

She showered, scrubbing mud stained hands, knowing she'd never get them properly clean. Finally, dressed in sober black, she piled her wayward red hair precariously on top of her head, crammed a black hat on top, took a deep breath and walked down the stairs at the front of the hotel with as much dignity as she could muster.

Emily, the hotel manager, stood in the entrance hall.

'Is everything ready?' Imogen asked.

'Yes, Mrs Bishop.' Emily looked pointedly at her watch. 'The funeral's due to start in fifteen minutes.'

'I'll be there. Just as well it's only a hundred yards down the lane.'

2

THE FUNERAL

'Champagne and mushroom vol-au-vents. Perfect.' The vicar, Helen Pickles, towered over every other woman, and most men, in the hotel lounge. She patted her substantial stomach. 'Hardly any calories at all.' She selected another morsel. 'Doctor told me to lose twenty pounds or my blood pressure would go through the roof. I told him I didn't mind meeting my maker sooner rather than later, and if he thought I was going to give up chocolate cake, except for Lent, he could think again.' She chuckled. 'And Lent has finished at last. I ate three Easter Eggs on Easter Sunday – thought I might not make it to Evensong.'

Imogen sipped soda water. 'Thank you for the funeral, today. It was... lovely.' That sounded inadequate. How should you describe a funeral?

The vicar smiled. 'All part of the service. Pity about the rain, but the hymns went down well, didn't they?' She selected another canapé. 'If you need a sympathetic ear while you find your feet in Lower Hembrow, I have two. Although one doesn't work as well as before.' She pulled at her left earlobe. 'What with the deafness and the blood pressure, and needing reading glasses, I'm falling apart.'

Imogen hesitated. 'I'm not sure about staying here, yet. I know nothing about running a hotel. I'm a gardener.'

Helen swallowed the vol-au-vent. 'A bit more than just a gardener. I saw that piece about you in *Somerset Life* last month. Celebrity landscaper, that's you.' She wafted a hand in the direction of the young hotel manager. 'Emily is the most efficient manager I've ever known, and I've met a few in my line of work. She'll keep The Streamside Hotel going while you decide what to do.' Her eyes were kind. 'I hope you stay, but, of course, it's your choice. Now, is that a plate of brownies I see over there? How can I possibly resist?'

Imogen moved from one group of her father's friends and business acquaintances to another, accepting condolences and making small talk. She tried to eat a canapé but couldn't swallow. Her throat ached with emotion and tension, but it wasn't just her father's sudden death that hurt. Money worries nagged at her. Why hadn't he told her he was broke?

He'd left the hotel to her, but it hadn't made a profit for years, so far as she could see. She hoped she'd misunderstood the accounts. She could barely afford the funeral director's bills, even with the commission from Haselbury House.

She joined Councillor Smith, her father's best friend, his bulbous nose even redder than usual as he mopped his eyes with a giant snowy handkerchief.

His short, plump wife stroked his hand and peered round the room with beady eyes that registered every guest. 'Lovely service,' she remarked to Imogen. 'I don't see your husband here. Your father spoke so well of him.'

Imogen stitched a smile on her face. 'I'm afraid Greg couldn't come. Work commitments, you know.' It sounded lame. She hadn't contacted Greg, not since they split up, but surely he'd known about the funeral – it had been a headline in the local paper. She'd expected him.

Mrs Smith sniffed. 'Such a pity. Still, a lovely service, don't you think, Eddie?'

Councillor Smith nodded. 'Aye, he deserved a good send-off, did Horace.'

Smith and Jones, Imogen's late mother had called the two men. Their sixty year friendship ended abruptly when her father's car skidded, landing in a shattered pile of glass, steel and chrome, upside down on the road just outside Camilton.

Should Imogen have visited her father more often, checking he was safe to drive at his age? It would have been a waste of time. When had her father ever listened to his daughter's opinion?

In recent years, she'd only visited the hotel at Christmas, to exchange wine and chocolates.

A discreet cough sounded close by. Imogen smiled politely at Councillor Smith and excused herself.

The man from the pub over the road – Hennessy, that was the name, Adam Hennessy – grinned and held out a laden serving tray.

'What are you doing here?' She stopped. That was rude. 'Sorry. I thought the hotel staff were serving, today.'

'I'm helping out. Your manager begged me to. She sounded desperate.'

And somehow forgot to mention the arrangement to Imogen.

Emily hadn't exactly welcomed her recent arrival with open arms.

Adam Hennessy's round, cheerful face beamed. 'I come free of charge.'

A hot blush started at the back of Imogen's neck and spread across her face.

'Not the right thing to say at a funeral. Come now, we're both in business. Weddings and funerals, all good for trade. Christenings and bar mitzvahs, not so much. Religion seems to be dying out, although our vicar seems to thrive.'

It was hard to resist the man's nonsense. He was... well, the word that sprang to mind was merry. The top of his head barely reached to Imogen's chin and his eyebrows sloped, like an imp's. Pale blue eyes twinkled behind thick horn-rimmed glasses, and his hair, white and sparse, stood in tufts, as though surprised to find themselves still attached to his scalp.

He could be a leprechaun, although a very English one. The idea made Imogen smile.

'Now, that's better.' He beamed. 'I always think a funeral should be a celebration of life, don't you?'

'Well, yes. I suppose it should.'

She added, 'Councillor Smith was in excellent voice in church. He's Welsh, of course.'

'And one of the local choir's best tenors. Not that I know much about singing – I have a sandpaper voice – but the choir's thriving. They drink in The Plough after rehearsals, and what a thirst they bring – they'll keep me from going bust.'

Imogen's self-control gave way with a crack of laughter.

Across the room, the mayor glanced her way, eyebrows raised. 'Lovely service,' he boomed, repressively.

'Lovely,' she muttered, choking back another chuckle. 'I'm sorry,' she told Adam, embarrassed. 'It's not funny. I mean, my father's dead. I think I'm getting a bit, you know...'

'Hysterical? Nonsense. You're having a normal human reaction to the funeral. That's why a wake's important – to lighten the load after the burial.' He looked closely at Imogen; eyes bright. 'Your father was famous around here. Quite the businessman.'

Was that a compliment? The glint in Adam Hennessy's eyes didn't entirely match his words.

'Anyway,' Imogen regained her dignity, 'thank you for helping out. It's much appreciated.'

He raised one of his peculiar eyebrows. 'The great and good of Camilton are here in force.' He jerked his head in the direction of the mayor, who stood four-square in the centre of the room, legs akimbo, telling his usual jokes to an appreciative audience of councillors.

'So I see. And enjoying themselves enormously.'

* * *

At last, stomachs full, heads awhirl with gossip, and cheeks glowing from the effects of wine, the guests raised a final toast to their old colleague and drifted away.

The sole female councillor, a rising star with hopes of moving into national politics, had allowed herself only one small glass of white wine. She kissed Imogen warmly on the cheek and patted her arm, but their eyes didn't meet.

'Your dear father set an example to us all. Let's do lunch. I'll ring you.'

Imogen smiled, hiding a twinge of cynicism. She doubted that phone call would ever materialise, for she had none of her father's clout in the area.

Adam Hennessy passed close by, winked, and whisked a tray of glasses off to the kitchen. Imogen followed.

'I'm sorry for your loss,' he said as he loaded the monstrous dishwasher. 'I should have said that, earlier.'

She tried not to squirm. He'd lived in Lower Hembrow for a year. He must know she'd hardly ever visited. The village grapevine would make sure of that.

'Mr Hennessy, please don't do any more work. You've already done far too much.'

'Call me Adam.' The grin transformed his face. He'd make a wonderful Santa Claus at the next Christmas party. If Imogen hadn't sold the hotel by then...

She nodded towards the grounds. 'Come and have a drink in the garden. It's stopped raining and the sun's come out at last. I could use some fresh air. Let's take some of my father's champagne to the orangery.'

'Do you grow oranges? Or maybe pineapples, like wealthy Victorians?' His eyes twinkled.

'Oranges, pineapples, limes – you name it and my father's grown it. He had green fingers and the grounds were his pride and joy. He loved gardening.'

'And you've inherited his passion?'

'That and his fear of spiders.'

Adam swept his arm over the view. 'You'll need a team of gardeners for a place like this.'

'Oswald, the head gardener, worked for my father for years. He's still here, though he must be in his late seventies. I hoped he'd come to the wake – he was invited, and I saw him in church...' Imogen led the way along the path that wound through her father's specimen trees.

The break in weather had not held, and rain set in again as they made their way to the orangery; that cold, driving rain that runs inside coats, soaks trousers and plasters hair to foreheads.

Imogen fumbled in a pocket. 'I keep the building locked. I've hidden my secret supply of cake here, to keep it safe from the hotel guests. My mother used to keep some in a corner cupboard behind the orange tree and I stocked up as soon as I moved in last week. Do you like fruit cake?' She twisted the key until the lock clicked, turned the door handle and pushed. 'It's stuck,' she grumbled, glancing at Adam. 'And I'm afraid you're soaked.'

Adam seemed unaware, his attention fixed, staring through the glass.

Imogen followed his gaze.

'There's something heavy there, stopping the door from opening. A tall box, or a bag...'

She pushed again at the door. It moved an inch.

Adam grabbed her arm. 'Stop,' he said. 'You'll hurt your shoulder. Let me.' He kicked, hard, and the door inched further open, the gap just wide enough to let him through.

Imogen followed close behind.

The bag moved, slid sideways, and collapsed on the tiled floor with a dull thud.

She gasped. 'It's not a bag. It's...' She took a step forward, but Adam threw out his hand.

'Don't touch anything.'

The man lay, fully clothed, slumped on the floor. His face was blank, eyes rolled back into his head until only the whites showed.

Adam crouched low, his fingers against the neck. 'We're too late.' He turned his head. 'Don't disturb the scene. Leave it for the police.'

Imogen's knuckles, pressed against her mouth in horror, muffled her voice. 'The police?'

Adam stood up, jabbing at his phone.

He talked, but Imogen did not hear a word. She was deafened by the roaring in her head.

'Greg,' she muttered. 'It's Greg.'

3

TEA

Adam mentally catalogued the scene, his senses on high alert. He'd seen many scenes of death in his thirty year police career, and he'd hoped never to see another, now he'd retired.

The sight would be fixed in Adam's head forever, taking its place with so many others. The orangery, crowded with plants, loomed over the slumped body, shielding it from the fading light. Adam could see no sign of a struggle, or an obvious weapon.

Questions queued in his head. Whose body was this? Why was it here, and why today? Was this suicide, an accident, or something more sinister?

The first was the easiest to answer. 'Greg,' Imogen had said. One of the guests had mentioned the name. Greg had been Imogen's husband.

Adam considered Greg's clothes; that leather jacket must have been expensive once. Underneath, a smart charcoal-coloured suit and a pair of shoes, claggy from the garden's red mud.

Greg had come dressed for the funeral. That suggested he'd died today, but Adam knew better than to jump to conclusions. He'd wait for the post-mortem.

But this isn't your case, he remembered. He could leave the investigation to the Avon and Somerset police. That was why he'd moved out here; to get away from police work.

It was impossible to switch off his instincts, though. Without moving, touching nothing, he let his gaze roam through the orangery, observing everything, determined to miss nothing. This would be his only chance.

The sun was fading fast, but light glinted from a nearby plant pot. Adam shone his phone on the spot. A bottle stuffed by its neck into the pot.

Champagne? Had Greg been drinking, plucking up courage to kill himself? Or maybe there were pills dissolved in the liquid?

Too much speculation. Stick to the facts.

A pang of guilt. He should be looking after Greg's wife.

Tearing his eyes away from the scene, he took a closer look at Imogen. One hand still clamped to her mouth, her cheeks paper white, she leaned against the orangery door, apparently close to collapse.

He took her arm. 'Come back to the hotel.'

* * *

Emily, with an efficient air and a smart, dark grey suit, her ash-blonde hair still neat, circled the hotel lounge, switching on table lamps.

The mourners had gone, at last.

A young waitress, hair escaping from a bun at the back of her head, stacked debris from the wake on a trolley: used plates, smeared glasses and empty cups.

Emily's eyes widened as Adam and Imogen lurched into the hotel lounge through the French doors, soaking wet and shivering.

'Is something wrong?'

'I'm afraid so,' Adam said. 'The police are on their way, and no one is to leave the hotel.'

Emily's red-lipsticked mouth dropped open. 'The police?'

'There's a body,' he explained, 'in the orangery.'

'My husband,' Imogen whispered.

The waitress dropped a bowl of sugar. With a sharp crack, it hit the edge of a table and fractured into three pieces. Grains of sugar flew into the air and fell, shimmering, on the hotel's best Turkish rug.

Adam said, 'Mrs Bishop has had a shock.'

Emily sprang into action. She shooed the waitress towards the kitchens. 'Fetch a dustpan, clear up the mess, and don't say a word to anyone.'

'Yes. I won't. I mean, I will... Sorry.'

'And leave the teapot.'

Emily recovered fast, retrieved clean cups from an oak sideboard, and poured tea with well-trained composure, only trembling fingers betraying her shock. 'Stewed, I'm afraid.'

Adam took a cup and helped himself to two large sugars. After one sip, he winced, laid it aside and explained where they'd found the body.

'We'd better get the staff and guests together. The police will want to see them.'

Emily nodded. 'I won't use the fire bell. I don't want to cause a panic.'

* * *

Imogen sat in the hotel lounge, on a squashy sofa by the fire, sipping cold tea while the police worked methodically through the staff and guests, taking names and asking questions.

They took pity on the young waitress, a teenager with saucer eyes, wrote down her details and sent her home as soon as possible.

Adam grinned. The cat was out of the bag, now that the girl was released. In half an hour, word would have spread and the whole village would know Imogen Bishop's husband had been found dead in the garden of her father's hotel.

He watched from the background as the police went about their business. Yellow police tape marked out the orangery and closed off the path to the car park. Light bulbs flashed and officers in protective suits moved in a practised ballet, searching for and securing evidence.

The long, depressing evening dragged into night as officials came and went until at last, in the early hours of the next morning, an ambulance removed the body to the morgue for autopsy and the police left, tasking a single, forlorn police constable to guard the crime scene, in a garden turned to mud by the combination of April rain and police boots.

Nothing, Adam knew, would be the same again for a long time.

4

MARIA

Adam scooped tinned mince into an old dish, his knees creaking. He must order dog food, or he'd be feeding this new arrival The Plough's best steak. The dog gazed at him with open mouth, panting with excitement. It looked like he planned to stick around.

'Adam, darling.'

Adam recognised the voice and his heart missed a beat. Maria Rostropova walked through his door, smiling. He wished she wouldn't do that. It did terrible things to his pulse rate.

A beautiful woman like this was out of Adam's league. He'd come to terms with that. Still, desire ambushed him every time he saw Maria. That smile, the hourglass figure, and the tip-tilted nose: perfection. Only a tiny scar running from the corner of her left eye and disappearing behind her ear spoiled the flawlessness of the exquisite face.

Adam had worshipped this woman from the moment they met four months ago. The local orchestra and choir, a motley collection of amateur and ex-professional musicians from the surrounding villages, had been rehearsing Christmas songs in the church and they'd built up a thirst.

'My good man,' the conductor had boomed. 'A pint each for the basses and tenors, and a glass of whatever they desire most, for our beautiful ladies.'

Warmed by Adam's best Hook Norton bitter, he'd taken a fancy to The Plough. 'We'll be back. Keep the beer on tap.'

They'd returned often. Free drinks guaranteed impromptu choral performances for the regulars and Maria's performance of 'Blow the Wind Southerly' could bring the drinkers to their feet in appreciation of her voice, by no means diminished by her personal charms.

Today, her eyes opened wide. 'That poor dog.' An Eastern European lilt enhanced the husky contralto. 'He's so thin. He must be starving. Where did he come from?'

'No idea,' Adam confessed. 'He's a stray – arrived yesterday. I wedged the door open this morning, but he wouldn't leave.'

'Is he chipped?'

'Can't tell. Unless someone claims him soon, I'll have to get the vet to run a scan. Otherwise, there's no chance of finding the owner.'

The dog trotted over to Maria, rubbing his head against her brightly coloured, floor length skirt. She knelt down, murmuring a stream of nonsense, like a doting aunt with a new-born baby.

She straightened. 'Let's not wait. Let's take him to the vet, now.' She clapped her hands. 'But first, I have a favour to ask, Mr Hennessy.'

Why the sudden formality?

'Adam.'

'Of course. Such a delightful English name. I came to beg you for help, Adam. You see, as you know, I sing in our choir.'

Adam nodded.

'I also chair the committee. We plan to give a charity concert in June, and we had this wonderful idea – why not play outside, with nature all around. In a field.'

'Why not?' Adam chuckled. He could see where this was leading.

'We were hoping to use the field behind the church, but there's been a little – how shall I say – difficulty. An objection. By the farmer. Something about trampling the crops. Poof!' Maria dismissed the farmer with a wave of the hand. 'We have to find an alternative, and we thought of your dear little beer garden. Would it not be perfect?' She smiled that adorable smile.

Adam was not fooled. Maria must have singled out the beer garden the first time she saw it. 'You'll be very welcome.'

'Adam, my darling. You are so wonderful and sweet.'

Adam had rarely been called sweet. He rather liked it.

'Now.' She clapped her hands again. 'Let's visit the vet. The dog will fit easily in your car, no? Mine has only just returned from the valet, and it would be such a shame to make it all dirty again, wouldn't it?'

* * *

The dog had no chip. The vet shook his head. 'He's a stray, I'm sure,' he decided. 'He looks as though he's travelled a long way. That makes me wonder...'

'Wonder what?' Adam asked.

'There's been a spate of dog thefts recently. Mostly high-end, working dogs – sheepdogs, show animals and such. Not scruffy mutts like this one.' He scratched the dog's chest and the animal leaned against him, hypnotised, eyes half closed in bliss. 'They were hidden in one of the farms north of here, up Hereford way, until it closed down a few weeks ago. Someone searching for a

Carpathian sheepdog found them and the police closed the place down.'

Maria shrieked with delight. 'I know Carpathians. They come from Romania, my home country. My uncle bred them on his farm.'

The vet laughed. 'I don't fancy you'll get your hands on that one – the owner was besotted by all accounts. Anyway, if they stole this fellow by mistake, they probably kicked him off the farm. They wouldn't want a mutt like him.'

Maria gasped; her hands clapped against the dog's ears. 'No, no. Stop saying that. You'll upset the poor creature. Won't he, darling?' She kissed the top of the dog's head.

The vet raised an eyebrow. 'He's most likely been wandering ever since. He's very young, hardly more than a puppy, and he's come a long way, but he seems in good health. Is he eating?'

'He could outdo a weightlifter,' Adam put in.

The vet looked at his watch. 'I must get on, I'm afraid. You should put a collar on this chap, if you're going to keep him, and a lead – this string won't last long. My nurse will show you.' He pulled out his phone to photograph the dog. 'I'll print this out and stick it up on the wall. It's a long shot, though.'

As they left, Adam had a brainwave. 'He might not be a Carpathian, but he's taken to you. Would you like to keep him?'

'Oh, I would love to,' Maria trilled, 'but I'm far too busy. I could never look after him as he deserves...'

Nice try. Adam shrugged. Maybe someone else in the village might adopt him.

He bought a selection of collars, leads, bowls, rubber bones, beds, and dog blankets from the vet's nurse, gasping at the range of items a single dog needed – and the price. He slipped the collar round the dog's neck, replacing the garden twine, and attached the lead.

'Looks like you're staying with me for a while, my friend,' he said, stroking the rough brown coat. 'Try not to shed hair all over the car seats.'

* * *

Back at The Plough, Maria slid from Adam's car, wiggled her fingers, and disappeared.

Adam heaved his new companion out of the back door, checked the lead was properly attached and retrieved the bag of canine essentials. He scratched his head. 'After all that, I forgot to buy your food. Fancy a walk to the shop?'

He didn't need to ask twice. The dog hauled him at speed along the lane and around the corner to the village post office, the Hembrow Stores.

Adam elbowed the door open and hovered. What about the dog? In or out?

'Come in, come in,' boomed Mrs Topsham, breaking into a loud belly laugh. 'What a super dog. Bring him in, do.' She squeezed round the counter, bounced across the room, bent over as far as her girth would allow, and threw her arms round the dog. 'Just what you need, Mr Hennessy, in my humble opinion. A bit of company.'

Panting with the effort, she straightened up and punched Adam heartily on the shoulder.

'As I was saying to Mrs Croft, only the other day,' she hooted, 'you need a companion. Not good for a man, living all alone.' She rocked with laughter. 'I wasn't thinking of a dog, mind you, but there aren't many ladies to choose from, not in Lower Hembrow, are there?' She kicked the door shut and trotted back to the counter, wheezing. 'Not unless you count Mrs Bishop.' One eye closed in a wink.

Better knock that rumour on the head. He opened his mouth to protest, but Mrs Topsham was on a roll.

'Not your type, I expect. A bit on the thin side, but that's what girls are like, these days.'

To Mrs Topsham, anyone younger than her was a girl.

'Poor thing,' she added, in a loud whisper. 'First, her father dies and then, on the day of the funeral – the very day, would you believe,' her voice rose to an excited squeak, 'there's a dead body found in the garden. Oh—'

The door opened, halting her in mid-sentence.

She recovered fast. 'Oswald, what can I do for you?'

Adam's dog almost pulled Adam over in his haste to get to the newcomer.

In her stage whisper, Mrs Topsham announced, 'Oswald's the gardener from the hotel. Bet he knows all about that body. Don't worry,' she put a finger to her lip. 'He's deaf as a post – can't hear a word.'

'Oswald and I are old friends,' Adam announced.

'Really?' sounding disappointed. 'Drinks in the pub, I suppose.'

The gardener looked up. 'What's that you say, Edwina? A tin of my usual, please.'

Puffing hard, she reached into a cupboard behind the counter. 'Time you gave up that old pipe of yours before it kills you,' she scolded. 'That or the beer. One of them will see you off, you mark my words.' She slapped a pack of tobacco on the counter. 'Come on, now. Spill the beans. We're dying to know about that body in the garden.'

'Aye, well, I wasn't there, was I?' the gardener said, with a sharp look at Adam. 'My day off yesterday, you see. I went to the church, to see the councillor off to his last resting place. Mrs Bishop asked me to that posh affair in the hotel, but affairs like that aren't for the likes of me – too many bigwigs from the town. I drank a pint or two to toast the councillor's memory at home with the wife.'

'Well, I heard,' Mrs Topsham piled cans of beans in a neat pyramid, 'the body was Mrs Bishop's husband.' Her hands stilled. 'What do you think about that, then? Mrs Croft told me when she popped in for a bag of sugar, first thing this morning, and she had it from the waitress's mother.'

The village grapevine had done its work.

Adam paid for his dog food and left.

5

PAINTING

The hesitant tap on Adam's newly repaired door sent the dog into a spin, galloping past Adam, sliding on the mat and whirling in excited circles in the tiny entrance hall.

'Mrs Bishop,' Adam nudged the dog aside and ushered his visitor into the sitting room.

'Do you mind?'

'Of course not. Come in, sit down and take it easy.' Imogen's eyes, ringed with dark shadows in her pale face, suggested a sleepless night after she finally turned in.

He left her in the more comfortable of his two armchairs and wrestled with the coffee machine in the tiny kitchen.

'Latte, cappuccino, or something called "macchiato",' he asked, sticking his head round the door. 'Whatever that is. This machine's new to me. Still, I think the coffee will be better than last night's stewed tea.'

Imogen rewarded him with a tense smile.

Light flooded through windows that reached from floor to ceiling. He'd left the door to the garden open, and the soft spring air filled the room. Outside, the stray dog lapped noisily at a bowl of water.

Imogen inhaled. 'Basil?'

'Well spotted. I grow other herbs as well – rosemary, thyme and so on. They're handy for recipes. But you know that – you're a gardener.'

'I like to get my hands dirty.' She held them out for inspection, the nails short, the skin roughened. 'As you see, I keep forgetting to wear gardening gloves.'

Imogen broke a short silence.

'I hope you don't mind me coming over – I'm not here for sympathy. Of course, I'm sorry Greg's dead, but we'd split up and the marriage was over ages ago.' She pursed her lips. 'That sounds callous. A liaison officer talked to me earlier today. She was so kind, I felt like a hypocrite. I hoped you might not judge me.'

Was that a compliment?

'I won't, but you might have to weather a bit of gossip. Have you been to the village shop yet?'

She grinned. 'Not since I moved back last week, but I can imagine. I bet Greg's death is a hot topic.'

'That and my new friend, this dog – both events of equal interest to the proprietor. She tells me I need a companion. A full bar every night isn't enough – and I don't think Mrs Topsham approves of drinking.'

She laughed. 'Useful warning. The dog's a new arrival, is he?'

'Picked me out. I've no idea why. I've never owned a dog in my life.'

By the time Adam finished the story of the dog's sudden appearance at The Plough, colour had returned to Imogen's face.

He risked a few questions. 'Sorry if I'm being nosy, but did your husband plan to come to your father's funeral? He was wearing a suit.'

'Not nosy at all. You discovered the... the body with me. You earned the right to know more.'

Should he tell her he used to be a police officer?

Too late, she was already talking.

'I didn't know whether or not he'd come. It was awkward – people asked when he'd be arriving.' She bit her lip. 'He was probably out there all the time, in the orangery – dead.'

'Where were you living?'

'I have – we had – a flat in Salisbury. It's up for sale, now.' She shrugged. 'I moved over to the hotel when my father died. It seemed right. I couldn't leave it without an owner, although I know precious little about the business.'

She managed a lop-sided grin. 'To be honest, I'll be glad to get rid of the flat. It's never been the same since Greg and I split up.'

Adam said, 'Do you have more family? Aunts? Grandparents?'

She shook her head. 'Not really. My father was the last of his generation. A couple of distant cousins live in the Lake District, but they couldn't get to the funeral.'

'What about friends?'

An odd expression flitted across her face. Guarded.

'Plenty of acquaintances – other gardeners, people in the business. Not close friends.' She drained her coffee cup and sat up straight. 'This is a great building. A Somerset longhouse, isn't it?'

'I keep this end for myself, and the bar and restaurant occupy the rest of the building. It works well.'

She pointed across the room. 'That painting over there?' She got up and moved closer. 'The one of the lake, with the rushes. It's the pool at The Streamside Hotel, isn't it? Local artists often used to paint it – my father was proud of the garden. Where did you get it?'

'You've discovered my guilty secret – it's one of mine. I'm a keen amateur – very amateur, I'm afraid. I paint in my spare time. Not that I have much of that, running The Plough.' He laughed, suddenly awkward. 'I'm a beginner. That's the only example of my work I consider successful enough to put on the wall. Your father let me play at painting the hotel gardens.'

'Clever you. I love the way you've suggested the light on the water.' She turned to face him. 'What did you do before you came here?'

Confession time. He braced himself. 'I was a police officer.'

'What?' Her eyebrows shot up.

'In my defence, I told the DCI last night.'

'Did you? I didn't hear.' She paced from the wall to the chair and back. 'Well, how very odd.' She trod the same route again. 'You must be bursting with curiosity about my husband, then,' she said.

'A little,' he admitted.

She took another turn round the room.

'Could you sit down?' Adam begged. 'You're making me giddy.'

She resumed her seat. 'Are you going to investigate Greg's death?'

'Not my job.'

'Come on. How can you resist? Why don't you ask me questions? Get them out of the way? Surely, you want to know whether Greg committed suicide, or whether he was murdered? I know I do. You might even think I killed him...'

She sounded calm. Was she angry? Hard to tell. He'd take her at her word.

'Very well, tell me about Greg.'

'I'll give you the unvarnished truth. It's depressing.'

He waited.

'Well, as I said, we'd split up. Unfortunately for me, he emptied our joint bank account at the same time. We'd quarrelled, you see, about three months ago. I had to work away overnight, starting up the Haselbury House project, and he objected.' She shrugged. 'To be honest, I think he was jealous, because I love my work and he was struggling.'

Her face cleared, as though she'd discovered an unexpected kernel of truth. 'Greg's business was under pressure. He sold various things across the south and west of England – different items he picked up cheaply – sometimes, I'm almost sure, off the back of a lorry. He travelled a lot and lurched from one business idea to another. I found it refreshing when we first married, but the businesses never prospered.' She rolled her eyes. 'His brand of feckless charm wore off years ago.' She moved the cup in its saucer. 'I've known for years that Greg had other women. He was,' she smiled, 'very attractive to women. I'd grown tired of pretending I didn't notice when he stayed out late, or when he took secret phone calls.'

She took a gulp from her cup. 'The final straw came when I found a receipt in his pocket. I wasn't even snooping – he'd asked me to put his trousers in the wash. I don't think he cared whether I knew or not. The receipt was from a jeweller.' Her laugh rang harshly through the room. 'Such a cliché. He hadn't bought jewellery for me for years. We had a huge row and told each other a few home truths. Apparently, I have a few personal faults of my own.'

She gave a wry smile. 'The next day, we were very polite to each other. I left to start work at Haselbury House, thinking we would both cool off and maybe patch things up, but he disappeared without even the courtesy of a note. When I came home next day, he'd gone, taking very little except his clothes and, as it turned out, our savings. He did love clothes.' Her smile was wistful. She'd obviously been fond of her husband once. 'He didn't, so far as I could see, keep any other reminders of our marriage.'

She rose and stretched. 'I promised to go the police station to give a statement – a bit more private than having more police in the hotel and I want a solicitor with me.'

'You don't need one at this stage.'

'Still – Greg would insist. He didn't trust the police.'

The stray dog rushed into the room.

She knelt down to the animal's level. He licked her face. 'Aren't you beautiful?' she murmured. She grinned up at Adam. 'I think you've made a friend.'

* * *

Adam's head buzzed with questions after Imogen left, but his fingers itched to paint. He'd come to this quiet backwater with its sleepy pub and rural views, planning to run The Plough and spend his leisure time painting. So far, the plan had worked. He relished the late nights of chatter, and didn't mind early starts, cleaning up after the night before. He had no ties, no wife, no partner, no children. No family at all, just slight regret that love had never blossomed. Or at any rate, had flared up only once, briefly, with a woman who'd used him as a meal ticket before moving on.

He'd never felt bitter. At least Yolanda had granted him a few months of one-sided affection.

He retrieved the last old canvas from under his bed and lugged it down to the sitting room.

Better pick up some more recycled canvases soon.

He loaded his brush with grey paint and smothered the

canvas with a wash, sweeping strokes overlaying the uncertain still life underneath, but for once, the magic wouldn't happen. His mind could not let go. Suspicions, questions, and observations whirled in his brain.

He put down the brush. Who was he trying to fool? He couldn't ignore a sudden death just across the road.

He cleaned his brushes, packed the tubes of paint in their box and reached for his phone.

* * *

James Barton, a forensic medical examiner from Adam's old days, yawned in Adam's ear.

Adam winced. 'It's Adam Hennessy here. I've picked a bad time, by the sound of it. You're on call?'

'Twenty-four hours on the trot – but I'm getting to the end of the shift. Don't expect any sense from me...' James stopped talking. When he spoke again, there was a note of curiosity in his voice. 'Haven't heard from you for a while. Not since... Well, how are you?'

Adam pictured James at home in bed, catching up on sleep, only half awake. 'Not as tired as you, at least. Busy time?'

James groaned. 'Two drunk drivers and a battered wife. Nothing unusual. What can I do for you?'

'It's personal, James. I was hoping to run some things past you. Face to face if possible?'

'No problem, if you'll come here. How about lunch tomorrow? The Slug and whatever-it's-called?'

'I'll be there.'

6

The Slug and Lettuce was one of a chain, situated in the middle of Birmingham, in an area Adam knew well. He shot a glance around the bar, automatically checking out the other drinkers. He could relax. No one he knew was in today.

He ordered a soft drink, and chose a table tucked away in reasonable privacy. The dog curled under the table, keeping an eye open for scraps.

'I thought you were a cat person,' James dwarfed the room as he burst in, bought a diet coke, scraped back a chair opposite Adam and collapsed into it. 'Good job they let dogs in here,' he said, as a young waiter arrived to take their orders.

Adam told the tale of the dog's arrival. 'You wouldn't like to take him on, would you?'

'Not me. I have enough bother from the kids.' He jerked his head at the rows of tables. 'Not quite like the pub you've taken over.'

Adam raised his glass. 'You've done your homework. Or the grapevine's still working. I haven't seen you since...'

'Since your retirement do. What a night that was, mate.' James had stuck with determination to his North London roots and the slang to match, although he'd lived in the West Midlands for over thirty years.

'Can't imagine you remember much about it.'

James snorted. 'True enough. But judging by the headache next morning, it was one of the best.' They paused as two plates of burgers and chips arrived.

James took a break from dosing his chips with salt and vinegar and smothering the burger with tomato sauce, to peer at Adam through narrowed eyes. 'You're looking good, Adam. Retirement suits you. You look twenty years younger, apart from the hair. That's still on the retreat, I see.' He slid one hand through his own carefully trimmed salt-and-pepper thatch. 'Anyway, tell me about your pub.'

'Sixteenth century, quiet village, not much happening. At least, not until yesterday.'

James' long, battered face creased in a smile. 'I smell a mystery. But first, what about you? You disappeared like a puff of wind; you know. Not a word for your mates for a year. We all thought you'd emigrated.'

'Well, you know how it was...'

'I remember.' James paused. 'Sorry about your cat.'

Adam nodded. That had been the worst part of the whole business. His beloved cat, an ancient tabby, his companion for more than sixteen years, had been the victim of a revenge attack by a gang of Cypriot thugs. Adam found the animal, throat slit, in a pool of blood on his living room carpet.

'Couldn't go on living there, so I sold up and bought the pub. No ties, you see. A taste of relaxed village life. Although, after yesterday, I'm not so sure it's as quiet as I expected.'

'Intriguing.' James wrinkled his forehead, black eyebrows

aloft. 'Oh, for the single life with no one to please but yourself. A pub of your own. I can only dream.'

'And how are the kids?'

'One word. GCSEs.' James' face fell.

'I'm not sure GCSEs counts as one word. Is it your youngest taking them?'

James raised his eyes to the ceiling. 'And the oldest is doing A levels ready for university so she can cost us a small fortune in handouts...'

'And Jenny?'

'Still a nurse manager, full of suggestions for how the government should be running the NHS. So, no change there.' James swallowed half his pint of Diet Coke in one mouthful. 'Can't wait to have a proper drink later. This stuff rots your teeth. Now, let's get to business. Is it a woman?'

'When is it ever a woman with me?'

'Right.' James grunted. 'Come on, man. Do I have to drag it out of you? You ring out of the blue and tempt me to this spectacularly unattractive hostelry, to eat burgers made from the worst bits of some poor animal's carcase. I assumed you had some juicy case to talk about.'

'I'm retired.'

'Of course, you are, and I'm a ballerina. You'll never retire, my son. You're a detective to the core.' He wagged a bony finger in Adam's face. 'That's why you wanted to meet in person – so you can watch my reactions. It's what you do. Body language, human behaviour, lies and secrets are your specialities. Now, spill those beans while I finish these chips.'

Adam told him about finding Gregory Bishop dead in the garden of the Streamside Hotel. James nodded and frowned, waving chips in his fingers. At the end of the story, he pushed his plate to the side, wiped his mouth and fingers, sighed and leaned his elbows on the table, his chin in his hands.

'So, this woman's husband left three months ago and she hasn't seen him since, or so she says, until he turns up on the very day of her father's funeral, dead.'

He raised his eyebrows and Adam nodded. 'That just about sums it up.'

'Well, what do you think is going on? Suicide? Accident?'

Adam swirled the last drop of orange juice and lemonade around in the bottom of his glass. 'Could be any of those things, but the suicide idea doesn't ring true. The man was dressed for a funeral, he was expected, but he never arrived. Would you put your suit on if you're planning to take pills and drink yourself to death in the garden? And wouldn't you leave some sort of note?'

'Not necessarily, although people usually do. And, it's hard to die by accident sitting in a posh conservatory. You said there was a bottle nearby? Are we talking poison, by any chance?'

'It's no more than a possibility. There are a few possible motives. According to his widow, Gregory Bishop has been involved in some shady businesses. He could have trodden on someone's toes once too often. Or it could be an elaborate attempt on his wife's part to get rid of her husband, hide the savings she claims he took, then come up with a perfect alibi and get away with it all.'

James hooted. 'Remind me not to get into crime while you're around. But Avon and Somerset's finest will be on the case. Why do you want to get involved? DCI Andrews; isn't he the local guy? Big chap, spectacular eyebrows? Bit of a plodder with one eye on retirement?'

'Truth is, I'm worried about the wife. She's a strong woman, but she's lost her father and now her husband. She's independent – won't even let the liaison officer help. I think she needs to have a few answers, and quickly. Always supposing she didn't murder her own husband.'

James finished his Coke, grimaced, and dumped the glass back on the table. 'Fancy her, do you?'

'N-no. I like her, and my gut tells me she's innocent, although the whole 'taking me to the orangery' thing could be an elaborate double bluff, I suppose. Still...'

'You have your eye on someone else? I knew it.'

Adam ignored that. 'I wondered if you could help – maybe pull a few strings, find the cause of death?'

'So you can solve the case for her?' His face the picture of lugubrious sorrow, James shook his head. 'Once a detective...' He checked the time, wiped his mouth and lumbered to his feet. 'I have to go. Don't leave it so long, next time, mate. I'll see what I can do.'

As his friend drove off in a mud spattered Range Rover, Adam pulled out his phone and googled the number of the local police.

He did not get through to DCI Andrews himself, of course. 'Please make a note that this is former DCI Hennessy calling.'

'Hennessy?' The young man at the other end of the phone sounded suddenly interested. Adam's heart sank. 'Not... not DCI Hennessy from the Andiron case?'

'Just pass on the message, lad.'

7

INVITATION

Imogen, the two police officers explained, was being interviewed as a witness. At least they weren't calling her a suspect. She braced herself, glancing at her solicitor for support. Sheila Brooks gave a half-smile, her lips tight as though gestures of sympathy did not come easily.

One of the officers, a young woman, said, 'Please tell us what happened on the day of your father's funeral in your own words, Mrs Bishop.'

Imogen wanted to laugh. Whose words did they think she might be using? She squeezed her hands until the nails dug into her palms to gain control.

'Mrs Bishop?' the officer repeated.

Imogen took a breath, and the interview began.

A male officer took copious notes, and in the corner of the room, the red camera light gleamed. They weren't going to miss a syllable of her story.

The female officer nodded, encouraging Imogen with an occasional, 'Go on,' and, 'What happened next?' Imogen's heart-beat slowed as she explained how they'd discovered Greg's body.

She'd been worrying about nothing, imagining the police were going to set traps for her. Maybe she'd watched too many police procedurals on television.

She sat back, relieved to reach the end of the story.

The policewoman glanced at her colleague. He gave a tiny nod.

'Now,' she said, 'tell us about the last time you saw your husband.'

Imogen's stomach lurched. She'd relaxed too soon. She licked dry lips and glanced at her solicitor, but Sheila Brooks chose that moment to turn a page in her notebook.

'Did you quarrel?' the policewoman asked, eyebrows raised politely.

The solicitor's head jerked up.

Imogen fought to stay calm. Should she tell the truth? Wouldn't that make her look guilty?

'No. It was a normal day. I went out early, to a stately home, Haselbury House. I was working in the gardens there. I planned to stay overnight, so I could work late and start early. They gave me a room...' her voice faded. That was too much information. 'Just answer the questions,' Sheila Brooks had advised.

The police officer nodded. 'Good. Now, did you speak to your husband, that morning, before you left?'

Imogen reflected. Greg had been asleep, waking only as she came back into the bedroom after her shower. He'd opened one eye. 'Make a cup of coffee, Immy,' he'd muttered, their quarrel apparently forgotten.

Imogen had no idea what time he'd returned home the night before. He'd slammed out of the flat after the row, muttering about going 'out with the boys'. 'Boys' was Greg's word for a bunch of men in middle age, every spare evening spent drinking beer together and arguing about football.

It seemed the previous evening's argument was forgotten. Imogen had bitten back a sharp retort and clattered round the kitchen, making coffee and toast. She'd left the food on a tray beside her husband.

He'd grunted.

She'd shrugged into a warm jacket. 'See you tomorrow night,' she'd called as she'd left.

'I made breakfast and said goodbye,' she told the officer.

'Did you kiss him goodbye?'

Imogen hesitated. 'No, I don't think so.'

'You can't remember?'

Imogen couldn't meet her eyes. 'Well, I didn't kiss him. I was in a rush. I grabbed my keys and ran.'

'You didn't kiss your husband, although you were going to be away for a couple of days. But you say you didn't quarrel?'

Imogen gulped. She opened her mouth to tell the truth, but before she could reply, the solicitor sat up straighter and sighed.

'My client has already answered your question.'

Imogen tried to breathe slowly. This was even worse than she'd expected. The police had lulled her into a false sense of security.

The officer took her through the story again, querying every detail. What had she been wearing that day? Where was Greg going? Had they spoken on the telephone?

Imogen tried not to squirm. She'd lied about her argument with Greg. The police couldn't know that, could they? It was too late to change her story.

She kept the rest of her replies simple, desperate to avoid more gaffes. The last thing she wanted was to be clapped in irons and led to a cell.

The tension mounted. Just as Imogen wondered whether her

head would explode, the officer smiled. 'That's all I need, for now. If you think of anything else, give me a call.'

Imogen stifled an urge to cry with relief. At least, she was still at liberty. She shivered. That was the only bright side. She must be at the very top of the police list of suspects, and she'd made matters worse by lying.

It took all her strength to make a dignified exit. At least the officers couldn't hear the thudding in her chest.

Her legs felt far too weak for driving. Maybe she should have taken the liaison officer up on her offer of transport, after all.

She would find somewhere to have a late lunch in town and give her body time to stop shaking.

The weather had suddenly turned unseasonably warm for late April, and Imogen's suit felt hot and constricting, her heels uncomfortably high. She tottered along the main street, past branches of Marks and Spencer and Boots, turning into the department store on the corner. The air-conditioning cooled her burning cheeks.

As she rode the escalator, her stomach rumbled. She'd be happy to eat sausage and chips. She needed a good dose of fried food this very minute.

Her tray loaded with artery blocking fat, she queued behind a woman bearing chocolate cake, blueberry muffins and a maple pecan slice. Someone needing a sugar rush. At the counter, Imogen ordered a cup of tea, craving a hot, dark brown brew, strong enough to stand a spoon in, as her grandmother used to say.

'Immy Jones. I don't believe it.'

Imogen swung round. The woman looked familiar.

Imogen stared, struggling to place her. Middle-aged, like Imogen, she wore an elegant light blue coat with style. Blonde-streaked hair curled around her cheeks. Imogen sucked in her stomach.

The name popped into Imogen's head. 'Toni Jackson.'

'That's me. How long is it since we bumped into each other? Must be thirty years.'

The boy behind the counter was waiting, hand on hip, foot tapping, for Imogen to pay.

'Oh, sorry.' She fumbled in her bag, dragged out her card and swiped it over the machine.

Toni Jackson said, 'Come and sit with me. I was just about to leave, but it's been so long since I've seen you...'

Hardly knowing whether to be pleased or horrified to meet Toni again after so many years, Imogen followed her across the room to a table overlooking a small park. She wished Toni had chosen a different table. From here, she could see the flat she'd shared with Greg.

Instead, she focused on Toni Jackson. They'd been in the same crowd at school. Never best friends, they'd rubbed along well enough. Toni – Antonia – Jackson had left Camilton to go to university and never returned, so far as Imogen knew. 'What are you doing here after all these years?'

Toni laughed, the low, gurgling sound Imogen remembered. 'My parents lived nearby, so I've been back a few times for a weekend, but my mother died and now Dad's got Alzheimer's. We're moving him into a care home, nearer to Birmingham.'

Imogen frowned. 'I remember your mother. She knitted your stripy jumpers. I'm sorry to hear about her – and your father. We're getting old, aren't we? My father died a few weeks ago.' Real tears threatened for the first time since her father's death. She rubbed at her eyes. 'I'm sorry. Oh dear.'

She scrabbled for a tissue in her bag, finding only old bills, furious at herself. She'd always been proud of her resilience.

When she was little, her mother had called her 'feisty' – her father, 'obstinate'.

Toni offered her a clean tissue, sliding a neat packet from her Mulberry bag. 'I saw the local news this morning. About your husband's death at the hotel. It must have been terrible, especially finding him yourself. I'm very sorry.'

Imogen fluttered her fingers, not yet ready to speak, horrified by her loss of control in such a public place.

Toni went on, 'It must be dreadful for you. Have you come out for a little retail therapy?'

Imogen sniffed. That made her sound like a hard hearted shrew of a wife. Still, better that than admitting she'd been with the police. 'Greg and I had split up,' she confessed. 'But it's been a shock, all the same.'

'Well, I know something that might cheer you up.' Toni took a pair of oblong reading glasses from a small case, settled them on her nose, extracted an envelope from the leather bag and read it aloud. 'Please come to a reunion of St Alban's school, class of '79. Bring family photos and anyone else who was there. Nisi Dominus Frustra.' Toni shrugged, 'Never did know what that Latin motto meant.'

'It's from a psalm. Something about not building things without God's help, I think.'

'I forgot you did Latin. Helpful for the names of plants, was it?'

Fancy Toni remembering she was going to study horticulture. 'Slightly.'

'Well, can you come?'

Imogen leaned across to see the date. 'I don't know. It's rather short notice. And with my father, and Greg...'

'Well, come if you can. I'm expecting Kate Lyncombe – remember her? And maybe,' her nose wrinkled, 'even Steph might make an appearance. It'll take your mind off – you know – Greg and everything.' Toni lifted her sleeve to examine a sleek, gold watch. 'Good Lord, is that the time? I have to go – an appointment with the estate agent. Selling Dad's house, you see. Those nursing home fees...'

In moments, she was gone, leaving Imogen puzzled. Had that meeting truly been accidental, or had Toni sought her out on purpose to invite her to the reunion?

She sat for a while, remembering her schooldays. Not the happiest time of her life, despite the popular saying. Her father, his business empire already growing fast, had sent her to a small public school full of wealthy girls from the minor aristocracy, with a smattering of doctors and lawyers' children. Imogen, tall, clever and self-contained, was one of a trio of friends.

For the first time in years, she missed the others – Kate and Steph.

She'd never been close to Toni, so extroverted and confident, wearing all the latest fashions to Queen concerts and Glaston-bury, and so full of confidence she'd hardly seemed to study at all for a place at university to study architecture.

After the exams, the small group had split up. They kept clear of each other. None of them had tried to meet – not after that one dreadful night, when their stupid escapade had gone so badly wrong.

Why would they want to meet now?

8

SCHOOL

Imogen retrieved her car and drove home, almost on automatic pilot. Meeting Toni had set off a series of memories she'd tried to forget.

A single day at school played, like a video, in her head. The sun had shone constantly that May. Imogen and her friends were about to take their A levels, and the weather had been gloriously hot. She'd sunbathed on the grass in the school grounds with Kate, her best friend, a maths student. Kate would be called a geek, these days, but the word hadn't been invented then.

The girls had stretched out under an ancient oak tree, pretending to revise for the upcoming exams, distracted by the weather.

'My knees are burning,' Imogen complained, trying to cover them with her bottle green uniform skirt.

'It's your fair skin. You shouldn't sunbathe at all.' Kate pushed across a bottle of Ambre Solaire.

Imogen read the instructions on the back of the bottle *Apply one hour before sitting in the sun.*

'Too late. I'll just have to put up with lobster legs and freckles.'

Kate's legs were beautifully smooth and brown. Imogen some-times wondered why Kate had chosen to be her friend. Petite, pretty, with ash-blonde hair that framed her face and swung gently in the breeze, Kate owned one of the brightest minds in the school.

'Hey, you two,' Steph Aldred plopped down beside the girls, hitched her skirt high and lay back on the grass. 'This is the life. I'm getting a suntan if it kills me. Budge over, Immy, you're blocking the sun.'

Imogen rolled obligingly onto her stomach. 'Serves you right if you burn.'

She stretched and yawned. 'It's far too hot to work, today.'

Steph threw a handful of grass at her friend. 'Who's working? I'm going into town. We need supplies for tonight.'

Imogen struggled to sit up. 'Tonight? I thought we were waiting until after the exams?'

Steph sniffed. 'People are starting to talk. Toni Jackson knows what we're planning. She grabbed me this morning and she wants to come along.'

Kate groaned. 'Trust her to get in on the act. Don't let her, Steph.'

Steph shook her head. 'We can't keep her out, now she knows, and we have to go tonight before she spreads it around. She's such a gossip.'

Imogen joined in, excited that the day had finally come. 'We can't trust her. If we wait, she'll tell everyone. Steph's right, we'll have to go tonight. What do we need?'

Their expedition had begun as a vague idea, conceived when their form tutor, Mrs Hall, lectured them on their first day in the sixth form. The basement of their common room, where supplies were stored, was strictly off limits. No one was allowed to venture down there.

According to rumour, a door in the basement opened on to a secret tunnel, leading under the hill to an old, ruined castle.

Steph, always adventurous, had sneaked down to the basement one morning when the whole school had been in assembly, and discovered the rumour was at least partly true. There was indeed a door, and it wasn't even locked. She'd pulled it open and discovered piles of books, paper and stationery.

Now, she chuckled. 'We need to bring the books and things out, then we can get into the tunnel. Good job Greg and Daniel and the others from the boys' school are coming. They can help.'

Kate pulled a sheet of paper from a file marked 'Applied maths' and started to read. 'Torches...'

'I bought those, last week.' Steph said.

Kate clicked her tongue. 'Don't interrupt.'

Imogen hid a smile. She'd known Kate for years, since primary school, but she could be a bossy madam.

She went on reading aloud, 'Food, the map – you copied it in the library, didn't you, Immy?'

Imogen nodded, and Kate continued.

'Sleeping bags, toothbrushes and wellingtons in case part of the tunnel is flooded.'

She finished reading and beamed at the other two.

'So, how many of us are going down tonight?' Imogen asked.

Steph pointed to each in turn. 'Us three – and now, Toni. And the boys, of course.'

Kate struggled to her feet. 'Well, she'd better bring some decent food with her, that's all I can say. Immy, how about some of that posh smoked salmon your dad serves in the hotel? Could you sneak some out?'

Steph giggled. 'I've never had smoked salmon.'

Imogen nodded. 'And I'll bring a bottle of wine if I can. Otherwise, it'll be cider.'

Steph rubbed her hands together. 'I've got a lesson in five minutes. Meet you all in the White House at 9 o'clock, and remember, don't tell anyone.'

If only they'd changed their minds.

9

ANDREWS

DCI Andrews' visit early the next day took Adam by surprise. The officer called at The Plough, unexpected and unannounced. 'I was passing.'

Seriously? No one ever 'just passed' Lower Hembrow.

'Gregory Bishop's death – I'd like to know more about the circumstances,' he began, as soon as Adam opened the door, not bothering with small talk.

'I gave a statement—'

'Your previous involvement with the police means you may have an insight or two.' Andrews spoke formally, through gritted teeth. 'As a courtesy, I came myself.'

'Not sure how much I can help,' Adam admitted.

He'd hoped for more fellow feeling. No doubt Andrews knew most of the details of Adam's last case. For a moment, he longed to discuss police matters, man-to-man, with someone who'd understand.

The DCI was talking. 'I can't share much information with you, Mr Hennessy, but I will tell you this. We've had a report from the medical examiner, who believes we have a deliberate poisoning on our hands.'

Adam instantly forgot his old case. 'It's murder, then?' He felt the old buzz of excitement. 'Any idea what poison?'

Andrews gave a bleak smile. 'Not yet. The pathologist won't commit himself this early on, of course, but preliminary tests suggest rat poison.'

'I'm sorry?' Adam blinked. 'Rat poison? I haven't heard of that for a while.'

'Turns out you can buy the stuff from Amazon. Brodifacoum, it's called. I think that's how you pronounce it. It's an anticoagulant and the victim died from internal bleeding. The medical examiner noticed some blood in the chest cavity and that gave him the clue.'

Adam took a moment to digest the information. 'Do you know when it was administered?'

Andrews shook his heavy head. 'There were traces in the bottle of champagne at the scene, so that's straightforward enough, and leaving the body in the orangery suggests an attempt to delay finding him. There was no key on him, by the way. Someone locked him in.'

Adam thought for a moment. 'It's easy enough for anyone to get into the hotel garden from the car park, which was full because of the funeral, so an alibi is going to be tricky.'

'That's an understatement.'

For the first time, DCI Andrews smiled. 'It's going to be a problem for the grieving widow, isn't it? Champagne from her hotel. Easy enough for her to slip the poison in, at any time, and give it to her husband.' He frowned. 'Haven't got a motive yet, but it shouldn't take long to find one.' He grinned, showing wolfish teeth, the first sign of informality. 'It's a miracle more people don't finish off their husbands and wives, if you ask me.'

Adam asked, 'Any detail on the time of death?'

'Sometime on the day of the funeral. That's the closest we can get at the moment. The grounds were closed off for the afternoon and the hotel guests given discounts on their bills. Clever move by that little manager. That explains why no one saw the body sooner.'

'Very clever.'

Whose idea had that been. Emily's or Imogen's?

'Did your men find anything useful at the scene?'

The detective looked at his watch, talking fast, as though he'd already wasted too much time. 'Nothing to speak of. Grateful if you let me in on any of your famous bright ideas. Might be useful.' He scowled, the brief moments of camaraderie over. 'We'll talk to Mrs Bishop again, soon.'

Adam watched him drive away, unsettled by the visit. Andrews seemed halfway to certainty that Imogen had killed her husband and keen for a rapid solution to the case. That was dangerous. Once an officer believed he'd found the killer it was difficult to maintain an open mind. Andrews' ego might prove to be a problem.

* * *

Adam planned a morning away from The Plough. For a few hours, he'd forget about Imogen Bishop, the crazy nameless dog that had adopted him, and Gregory Bishop's murder.

The sun shone and he had an appointment with his old friend, Henry, the owner of a Yeovil art gallery.

His own work would never merit gallery space, but Adam found relaxation wandering through Henry's finds. Occasional paintings touched a chord with their beauty. More often, he shook his head in wonder at the weird art people bought. Where did they hang these things? Could they stare at vast slabs of colour while they ate without indigestion?

Give me a Turner or a Constable, any day.

Henry, ruthless with his buying mistakes, had told Adam he wanted to unload a job lot of unsaleable canvases currently cluttering up his storeroom.

'I need the space. You can have 'em for peanuts. Cheaper than new canvases.'

Adam doubted that. Henry's haggling was legendary.

There was one obstacle to Adam's plan to visit the gallery. What should he do with this dog? He could hardly let it loose among Henry's canvases. He cringed at the chaos his new friend could wreak.

What did proper dog owners do when they went to work? Wasn't it cruel to leave an animal alone?

Racked with guilt, he ushered the dog into his sitting room, placing a bowlful of dog food on layers of old towels. 'Twice the price of corned beef,' he muttered. 'Hope you enjoy it.' He added a larger bowl of water. 'You be good,' he warned, without much hope. 'I'll be home soon.'

It was a mistake to look behind as he left. The dog's tail twitched, his huge brown eyes pleaded, but Adam hardened his heart.

'Stay,' he commanded, closing the door.

Throughout his drive to the town, a new doggy smell filled Adam's car, adding to the guilt. Amazing how fast a dog can infiltrate your life.

The hour in the gallery was meant to be an oasis of calm, far away from dead bodies, snooty police colleagues, and stray animals. The gallery owner, however, had other ideas.

Henry, corpulent, irrepressibly cheerful and expensively dressed, had heard of the 'Murder in the Hotel', as the newspapers had dubbed the death of Gregory Bishop. 'Don't you live in Lower Hembrow?' he accused as Adam walked in. 'Where people die in conservatories?'

Adam hesitated.

'Come on, spill the beans. Any theories?'

'Not yet. Probably an accident – drink and drugs, maybe. I'm retired, remember. It's none of my business. I'm enjoying a quiet life.'

Henry peered into Adam's face. 'Oh yeah?' he said. 'In that little backwater? I'll give you six months and you'll be longing for the city life. You'll go stir crazy in that part of the world, where nothing ever happens.'

'Apart from the occasional unexplained death?'

Henry laughed, jowls wobbling. 'Apart from that. You never know, it could be a murder.'

'Unlikely.'

Henry's face fell. 'Pity. I was hoping for some decent gossip to give the wife this evening. Otherwise, what are we going to talk about after forty years? *EastEnders*?' He gave a theatrical shiver. 'At least that *Poldark*'s finished. All the wife could talk about was the guy's six-pack. At her age! And me with my party seven. Ha, ha.' Henry slapped his stomach. 'Now, I was going to sell you a few canvases at mates' rates, that's right, isn't it?'

Adam scratched his head. 'You tried the mates' rates thing on me once before. I ended up paying over the odds. Let's set a fair price, shall we?'

They haggled for a while, finally agreeing a price, toasting their success with a bottle of Wilkins cider.

'Any masterpieces amongst this lot?' Adam flicked through a dozen leaning against the wall. 'Seriously, you couldn't sell this?' He picked up a canvas with two red squares set at jaunty angles.

'Funnily enough, no. Here, wait a minute,' Henry yanked out

a large painting from the back of the pile. 'I'd forgotten about this one. It'll interest you.'

The painting was stylised. The bird's-eye view, as though painted from the air, showed a series of small gardens, formally laid out in the Tudor style, with box hedges marking out geometric rectangles and circles. A straight, placid rill of water cut through from top to bottom, ending in a fountain.

'It looks familiar,' Adam leaned closer. 'I wonder if I've seen the setting. It's hard to tell – places look different from above. Is it a stately home?'

Henry guffawed. 'Nope. It's the garden where they found that chap. What's it called – the River Something Hotel?'

'Streamside.' Adam considered. 'So it is. I should have recognised it; I've tried to paint it myself. Any idea whose work it is?'

Henry shook his head. 'I picked it up for pennies, just for the canvas.'

'To sell on and make a killing out of saps like me...' Adam twisted his head to one side until he understood the angles. He squinted at the signature, but it was smudged and almost unreadable. 'Is that an F?' It was dated 1975. 'Painted a while ago. The place looks different, now.'

'There's another like it, in the back. Give me a minute...' Henry wandered away, puffing and panting out of sight. 'Got it,' he called, emerging with a red face and a smaller painting. 'This isn't oils. It's a watercolour, by the same chap, whoever he is. I took it on years ago, from another gallery.' He named a price, holding the painting out as Adam nodded. 'Mind you,' he mused, 'maybe I should hang on to it. The value's about to go through the roof, now the hotel's notorious.'

'Too late,' Adam grabbed it from his friend's hands. 'It's mine.'

This canvas was small and square, and seemed unfinished.

The artist had sketched in the geometry of the garden, but focused, with vivid, lively brushstrokes, on the central flowerbed.

'Nice little work, a bit Monet in feel,' Henry said. 'Pity the artist never finished it.'

'Any more like this?'

Henry grunted. 'No. I'd forgotten about this one, to be honest.' He glanced at Adam's face and grumbled. 'Can't believe I'm letting you have it at that price. More fool me.'

10

ORCHID

Adam struggled from the car, arms full of canvases, and turned his key in the lock. An ear splitting salvo of barking assaulted his ears. He'd forgotten his four legged companion – even getting used to the doggy smell in the car.

Warily, he pushed the door open and the animal leapt up, drooling, paws on Adam's chest, as excited as though his new owner had been away for a week.

Devastation met Adam's eyes. Scratches raked the wood panel of the door to the bar. Its handle bent at an angle, but the door had held.

Adam hardly knew where to begin. A nearby cushion, chewed to a mush, had sent its feathers flying across the carpet. A vase lay nearby, water seeping from it in a brown rivulet. Bare stalks had been tossed aside, and several flower heads had disappeared. 'Hope roses aren't bad for dogs.'

The dog's feeding bowl lay upside down, licked clean.

'How did you do all that so fast?' Adam demanded.

The dog lifted one paw.

'You think that'll get you out of trouble?'

Adam mopped and tidied as best he could, stood back and considered the dog.

'I suppose you were bored. Sorry, old chap. My fault.'

He attached the lead, an overpriced purchase from the vet, and gripped it securely.

'We'll show my new paintings to our neighbour.'

Panting, tongue lolling from his mouth, the dog trotted beside Adam as he staggered across the road to The Streamside Hotel.

Imogen looked thinner, her face more lined, but she greeted the dog with pleasure. 'Hello, lovely. Is he treating you well?'

'I'm at my wits' end,' Adam confessed. 'He's adopted me, and he's a friendly fellow, but he's wrecked my sitting room.'

'Did you take him for a run this morning?'

'No.'

She raised an eyebrow.

'I was planning to take him to the shop, later...'

'That's not enough. Mrs Topsham's is only just around the corner. He needs proper exercise. Look at him, he can't stand still – he's bursting with energy.'

She looked a fraction less tense than last time Adam saw her, but he knew better than to make guesses about her real feelings. In his experience, the worst killers often pretended to be devastated, while innocent family members could be too shocked to show emotion.

'He can run around the garden here,' she offered. 'There are gates and fences round the grounds, so he shouldn't get out. Unless he can open gates?'

'Wouldn't put it past him,' Adam muttered.

'My father kept dogs here, but the last one died a few years ago.' She led the way through the hotel lounge, and out of the French doors. 'What's his name?'

'He doesn't have one.'

'That's terrible. You'll have to think of one.'

'Trouble? Wrecker?'

Laughing, Imogen stooped to let the dog off his lead. 'Wow, look at him run...' The animal shot across the field towards the stream. 'He's going to need long walks. Twice a day.'

Adam changed the subject. 'The police have left, then?'

'They took down the tape this morning, while I was out. We can use the garden again, which is a relief, and I've reopened the hotel for bookings. The guests who were here then – you know, that night – they've all left. Couldn't wait to spread the gossip, I imagine. I'm dreading reading the online reviews.'

'I think you'll find business booms. Nothing more exciting than a hotel where someone died.'

'That's a bit morbid.'

'Sorry.' Adam winced. He'd been careless. Imogen's husband was dead. OK, she was a determined lady, in control of herself, and she hadn't collapsed in a heap at his death, that was admirable, but no matter how she tried to play down her feelings, those extra lines on Imogen's face told their own tale of shock and loss.

The police had allowed the crime scene to be closed. They must be sure there was no more evidence to be found there. No more fingertip searches, then. Was DCI Andrews jumping to conclusions? No need to suggest that to Imogen. She was under enough strain.

She broke into his thoughts. 'What were those paintings you brought?'

'They came from a mate of mine – a gallery owner. I thought you'd be interested in the subject. It looks like the hotel garden. I've left the paintings behind the reception desk. The very attractive young lady with multicoloured nails offered to look after them for me. Shall I set them up in the lounge? I think you'll be interested, and we can keep an eye on Wrecker while we look at them. Otherwise, he'll eat everything he can find. He's already mangled a couple of cushions and I suspect he had a go at the corner of my sofa.'

'Good idea – but please don't call him Wrecker.'

Her face became animated when she mentioned the dog.

Adam smiled, secretly. He had an idea.

* * *

The paintings rested, side by side, on two chairs, the watercolour glowing in the sunshine. 'The light's good in here.'

'It's even better in the orangery. You could paint in there, if you like. Not yet, perhaps. Soon.' Her smile was tentative. 'You're right. These are both paintings of the hotel garden. Artists often came when I was younger. It made my father feel like a proper landowner, I think. Sometimes, whole groups of amateur painters spent the day in the garden, and I would sit and watch. They gave me a little board – you know, one you can put your thumb through to hold it. What are they called?'

'Palettes?'

'That's it. I'd try to paint on an old bit of canvas. I used to make a wonderful mess. No talent at all.' She laughed, a proper hoot, the first Adam had heard from her. 'I used to know a real artist,' she mused. 'Daniel Freeman, that was his name. He didn't always use oils. Sometimes, he used to paint the flowers in watercolour, like in that painting...'

She fell silent, a thoughtful frown creasing her forehead. Adam waited.

She muttered, half under her breath, 'In fact, I wonder if that's one of his?' She picked up the smaller canvas and scrutinised it, talking almost to herself. 'He'd just left school. He was only a couple of years older than me, but he seemed grown-up, like a proper artist.' A touch of pink lit her face.

Was Daniel important to her? 'Did you keep in touch?' Adam asked.

'What? With Daniel?' She looked up and the happiness faded away. 'He came that last summer, just after I left school, before I went off to university. He was a student, at St Martin's in London, I think. When I... Well, he fell out with my father and left without saying goodbye. I never heard from him again. Then, I married Greg. He'd been at the same school.'

Adam let the silence spin out as she inspected the picture.

'Do you know,' she said at last, 'I think this could be one of Daniel's. His last name was Freeman. That could be an F, above the date, couldn't it? He sat in the formal garden for hours, sketching the different flowers. Of course, I didn't know what they were, in those days. I would now, I think.'

'Tell me?'

She grinned. 'Let's see. Here's a peony and some campanulas. We have plenty of those here. Pink and blue – they work well together. I'm not sure about this purple flower – oh, wait, it's an orchid But – oh!'

Her intake of breath surprised Adam. He'd been idly watching as the sun moved lower in the sky, enjoying the scent of lavender and rosemary drifting through the open doors.

'What have you found?'

She pointed to a tiny, bright flower, almost hidden behind the lush foliage of a plant that even Adam recognised as a hellebore. 'That's so rare. How could we have one of those in the garden? I'm sure it's a Gold of Kinabalu – amazingly uncommon, especially in England. It comes from Malaysia. One specimen would be worth thousands of pounds.'

She looked up. 'My father collected plants. He should have

been born in the nineteenth century. He would have loved to be a Victorian plant expert, travelling the world in search of exotic flowers. As it was, every time he went abroad, he returned with a new treasure. You're not supposed to do that, these days, because of the risk of introducing pests and diseases, but no one seemed to worry, back then.' She ran a finger over the surface of the painting. 'This orchid is different. He couldn't have found it growing in the wild. It would have been protected...' She paused. 'I wonder where it came from.'

'He must have bought it.'

She shook her head. 'I haven't seen any documentation. There should have been something in his desk if...'

'If he'd come by it legitimately.'

'Nonsense. Of course, he bought it. I just never knew. But then, I didn't come here for years.'

'Is it still growing in the garden?'

'I'm sure it's not. I'll go and look, later, but I'd have noticed. I've spent a few hours in the garden since I moved in.'

Adam was still peering at the painting. 'Any other valuable plants shown here?'

'I wonder about those snowdrops. There's quite a market in them, you know.'

'Surely they wouldn't be in bloom at the same time as this – what did you call it?'

'The Gold of Kinabalu. You're right, they're completely out of sequence. Isn't that odd?'

'Maybe he was just painting the plants he liked, without worrying about looking at them for real.'

'Mm.' She looked thoughtful. 'So, they might not have been in the garden at all. That makes more sense. Daniel just liked making gorgeous pictures.' She stepped towards the door. 'I'd offer to show you the whole garden, but it's just about to rain.'

She shuddered. 'Again.' She pulled her jacket closer. 'Can I take a photo of this painting? I'd like to identify all the plants. It will give me something to do – take my mind off things.'

Just then, the dog bounced into the room, mud on his nose. 'You've been digging,' Adam accused. 'You're a disgrace.'

Imogen put the painting down. 'You'll have your hands full with this dog. Bring him over, any time he needs a run. He can help me in the garden.'

'If you really mean it?'

'I do. He'll be good company. But first, you have to give him a proper name. "Disgrace" just won't do.'

Sure enough, it was raining again as Imogen sat down at her desk. Fat drops trickled down the window, blurring the garden from view. She craved the outside, yearning to get her hands dirty, but she'd have to wait. She grimaced. The ground would be soaked through.

Armed with coffee and biscuits, she settled down to research. She needed to know more about the rare plants in the painting. She piled gardening and botany books beside her desk, and flicked through their pages.

It was difficult to stay focused. Many of her books were old friends that had lived with her for years. Scribbles on the pages, handwritten notes and the line drawings in margins were all familiar, taking her back to hours of exam revision. Later books dealt with landscaping and architecture, reflecting her ongoing training for her profession.

Younger people would laugh, she knew, at the very idea of leafing through heavy hardbacks, when phone apps could recognise and name plants from photographs. In Imogen's eyes, they'd never replace the joy of thumbing through her own books, each page crammed with memories.

She clicked her tongue, annoyed. She was wasting time. She set the familiar texts aside and turned to the weighty glossaries from Kew gardens, and encyclopaedias from the Royal Horticultural Society. If the plants existed, she'd find them between those pages.

And there they were.

Her heart sank. The pictures confirmed her worst suspicions. The golden beauty, Gold of Kinabalu, was protected, and found only in Malaysia's Kinabalu National Park. For her father to have an example, it must have been stolen. Surely, he knew that.

'Oh, Dad,' she whispered. 'What were you up to?'

She found others, too. An intensely rare pygmy Rwandan water lily, the smallest water lily in the world, growing in hot mud at Kew Gardens, had been stolen years ago. It was tiny, but after squinting until her eyes hurt, she discovered one in the painting.

If an example had existed at the hotel, it incriminated her father. She hoped he'd done nothing more sinister than spend ridiculous amounts of money on rare plants, simply for the love of them. That would be understandable, if illegal – handling stolen goods was a crime. She sighed. Even if he'd paid for them, he'd surely know the plants had been stolen.

She sat back, face creased in thought, as she searched for another explanation, re-reading the conditions needed for growing the water lily. The grounds at The Streamside Hotel featured plenty of mud, especially today, but it certainly wasn't heated to the seventy-seven degrees Fahrenheit the plant needed.

A different thought struck her. Perhaps the artist – Daniel – had added plants to the painting that could never have been there?

The seed of hope grew. Her father may have been innocent. Perhaps he'd asked Daniel to include flowers he'd love to own.

The next step had to be his desk. If she found a legitimate invoice or receipt, she could relax. It would prove her father had bought the plants through legal channels.

She'd already glanced through it once, soon after he died. In the first trawl, she'd found one or two private letters amongst the Christmas cards from friends, acquaintances and other councillors.

Once again, she read the letter from Imogen's mother to her father, before their wedding. 'The man I can't wait to marry,' her mother had called him.

Imogen set it aside, stroking the paper with one finger. She'd keep it safe. It helped to know her parents had been truly in love. Her father couldn't have been all bad, if someone like her mother had loved him.

She searched again, for any trace of buying or selling plants, but found none.

Once more, she skimmed through the hotel's accounts. The place was definitely in trouble. Well, she'd discovered a possible reason. Perhaps her father's money had disappeared into the pockets of unscrupulous plant thieves.

Suddenly light-headed, she could hardly remember what she was trying to prove.

She neatened the piles of paper and slipped them into a fat filing box. Her father was dead, and safe from prosecution, whatever he'd done. But Imogen knew she couldn't leave it there. She had to know more.

11

BILLS

What should Adam do with this dog? He knew so little about the creatures. They leapt and bounced, knocking things off tables with their tails, tongues hanging out, dribbling.

Cats were so much easier to deal with. Augustus, Adam's ancient tabby, had been self-sufficient, his only demands a ready supply of food and water and easy access to the outdoor world. The truth, Adam had to admit, was that he missed Augustus. Maybe that was why he'd let this dog into his life – in the vain hope of filling an Augustus shaped hole.

This dog had a few good points, it was true. He was friendly, for one thing, and his big, brown eyes gazed at Adam with a heart-warming expression. On the other hand, he'd ruined Adam's sofa, peed on the carpet and shed rough hairs everywhere. And no matter how often Adam attached a lead to the brand new collar, and let the dog drag him round the village, the creature showed no sign of tiring. At this rate, Adam would be walking for hours every day – and he was longing to paint.

'Come on, then,' he sighed.

The dog galloped to the door.

Maria Rostropova's car drew up outside as they left. She leaned, waving, from the window.

'May I walk with you?'

'I was taking this creature across to the hotel. Mrs Bishop knows about dogs. I planned to ask the vet to find him a home, but I weakened.'

Maria jumped from the car, her face a picture of horror. 'Nonsense. You can't possibly do that. He's come to you. It's karma. It means he's chosen you and he's your responsibility now. Come, both of you, walk with me.'

Adam had no choice, for the dog trotted behind Maria, eyes fixed on her as though on a goddess. He gave the lead one last, hopeless twitch, trying to persuade the animal to cross the road to the hotel, but the dog was determined. Adam, with no intention of staging a tug of war in the middle of the village, gave in as gracefully as possible.

Maria chattered in her charming, broken English, waving at every passer-by and stopping to plant a kiss on the cheek of one lucky man. 'My gardener,' she confided to Adam, fluttering her fingers in the air. 'He charges me so little...'

Adam tried to imagine Imogen Bishop kissing one of her staff in lieu of payment.

'Now, my darling Adam,' Maria had taken his arm. 'Let's make the arrangements for our wonderful concert in your, er, what do you call your garden?'

'A beer garden.'

'Ah.' Maria patted his hand. 'Perhaps we could call it something else. A musical space, perhaps. You do not...' She stopped and turned to look Adam in the eye. 'You do not have those horrid gnomes in your garden, do you?'

With a straight face, Adam shook his head. 'No gnomes.'

'Good.' Maria walked on.

'When were you thinking of staging the concert?'

'Shh.' Maria held up a finger. 'Wait. A wonderful idea has come to me.' She shrugged. 'Now, this Mrs Bishop from the hotel. Perhaps she would like to be part of the event? After all, she has lost her father and husband. I feel we should be kind to her – make her welcome in the village. Don't you agree?'

She turned her radiant smile on Adam. 'Perhaps she could supply a little food from her kitchens. The publicity would be wonderful, and she will be worried about the business.'

'She will?'

'Of course, she will. Who would want to come to a hotel where people die?'

The last word, delivered in a deep contralto, was accompanied by a dramatic sweep of the arm.

'Still, if you think it a bad plan, I will forget it. I always listen to you, my dear Adam.'

He rather doubted that. Maria's head always seemed full of her own plans, leaving little space for the opinions of other people. Did she make use of Adam? Of course, she did, but he could forgive her everything when she smiled at him.

They walked on in companionable silence, until they turned a corner and a black-clad figure appeared. Maria gave a sharp intake of breath, her grip on Adam's arm tight.

'Councillor Smith,' she hissed.

Adam recognised one of Councillor Jones' old friends. The man had thoroughly enjoyed his old friend's funeral, so much so that he'd been forced to lean on his wife's arm as he left, cheeks purple-blotched from his champagne intake.

'Good afternoon, Mrs Rostropova.' The councillor nodded briefly at Adam, but his gaze remained fixed on Maria. 'How good to see you again.'

Ice sharpened Maria's voice. 'Good afternoon.'

She tried to walk past the man, but he stepped sideways, blocking her path. 'I believe we have some business to attend to. I was expecting to see you in my office, yesterday.'

'Oh, Councillor,' Maria, her tone warming, fluttered her eyelashes. 'It completely went out of my head. So many dreadful things have happened, lately. The funeral of poor dear Horace upset me dreadfully.'

'Poor Horace indeed,' the councillor nodded, briskly, 'but business is business, dear lady. I will tell my staff to send another appointment. I look forward to seeing you then.' He shot a sharp glance at Adam, commented, 'Nice dog,' and walked away.

Hair on the back of the dog's neck had risen.

'Well,' Maria fanned herself with one hand. 'That one is not – how do you say it – not gentlemanly. Not at all.'

Adam licked his lips. 'Are you in trouble, Maria?' he began, but she waved away his concern.

'Poof. The man cares only for business. Horace found him quite impossible.'

Horace? How close had Maria Rostropova been to Imogen's father? Was there some relationship between the two?

Adam said, 'Councillor Jones – Horace – was a friend of yours?'

'Oh, yes.' Maria had regained much of her self-control. 'A friend. Nothing more, of course.' Her cheeks bore a delicate pink flush. 'Now, dear Adam, let us discuss our wonderful musical evening.'

'In a moment. First, I need you to tell me a little about Horace Jones.'

She tossed her head. 'What do you want to know? We had a wonderful rapport. We shared a few projects...'

'Business or pleasure?'

Her tinkling laugh sounded strained.

'Come, Maria. If you are in difficulty, let me help.'

She walked in silence for a few yards. 'Very well, I will tell you. My old friend, Horace, helped me out with a small loan. You see, I had, perhaps, extended myself a little too far. My cottage is so beautiful. So English. But the roof – oh, I had no idea how much a thatched roof would cost. I bought the cottage with money left to me by my dear departed second husband, but then the bills began to come in.' She sighed. 'How can I, a poor immigrant widow, be expected to understand English ways? The thatcher was a villain. A villain – he told me the job would cost this much,' she held up her hand, thumb and forefinger a fraction of an inch apart. 'Then, when the work was under way, he told me it would cost this much.' Her hands moved a few inches away from each other. 'Finally, he refused to finish the work unless I paid a bill – a ridiculous bill, for this much.' Her voice rose in a wail, her arms held a full yard apart.

She leaned her face close to Adam, brilliant blue eyes sparkling with unshed tears. 'He is a crook, that workman. And what is worse, I discover he works for that man.' She pointed to the corner around which the councillor had disappeared. 'Yes, Adam, I owe that man money. Luckily, my friend Horace Jones helped me out. He was a gentleman. He loaned me enough to pay some of the bill, but that terrible man—'

'Councillor Smith?'

'Yes, the beast, he still wants more money.'

'That you owe him. For the building work?'

Maria slipped an elegant hand into her clutch bag and extracted a delicate lace handkerchief, with which she dabbed at her eyes. 'A little. I owe a little, but if I cannot pay, he will sue me for so much I will have to sell the house.' She sighed tragically. 'And then, I will be homeless.'

Adam nodded. 'And this musical evening – which you want me to hold on my land – will be used to pay off your debts?'

Maria shot him a glance under her lashes.

He sighed. She was very beautiful, despite the lack of moral scruples.

'Only a little. Most of the money will go to charity, of course.'

He interrupted. 'All of it, my dear. If I let you use my land, I will handle the receipts.'

Her face fell. She shrugged. 'Very well, dear Adam. I will give everything,' she waved one arm in a dramatic, sweeping gesture, 'everything to my charity.' She dabbed again. 'I will have to leave my home, unless I can raise the funds.'

'Have you tried a mortgage?'

'How can I? I have so little income of my own.' She placed one hand on her heart and whispered, 'I will be destitute, Adam.'

Fear shone in her eyes.

He took her hand. 'I'll see what I can do. But I won't break the law. Let me think about it.'

They turned and retraced their steps. As they reached The Plough, Maria planted a soft kiss on his cheek and Adam inhaled a gust of intoxicating perfume.

She drove away, anxiety wiped from her features. Her troubles were over now she'd found another man to solve her problems.

Adam shook his head. If only she were less beautiful, the tilt of her head less charming, her figure less enticing. His pension was enough for his needs, now the pub was thriving. If he chose to lend money to a lovely, feckless woman who enchanted him and let him pretend she cared for him – well, who could blame him; even if he never saw it again.

12

Adam was on his knees in the back room, grimly mopping up a trail of water left across the floor, when Imogen knocked at the door.

'Come in.' He beckoned with one hand, still gripping a wet tea towel in the other. 'This dog is nothing but trouble.'

The animal greeted Imogen with a rush of open-mouthed enthusiasm. Rising on his hind legs, he planted his paws on her shoulders, almost sending her flying.

'Down.' Adam's voice was stern. He glared, as fiercely as he could, and the dog subsided. 'Get back,' Adam went on, waving the damp tea towel towards the tiny back porch. 'Get in your bed.'

Adam fiddled about with coffee while Imogen sank into one of his chairs.

'You know,' she said, 'this is more comfortable than any in the hotel. They were chosen for appearances. They look squashy, but once you're in, it's a struggle to get out.'

'It stops the patrons leaving. Good for business.'

She gave a peal of laughter. Adam liked the sound. She hadn't laughed much, so far. Not surprising, really. Finding your husband dead in the garden would knock anyone off balance.

Adam allowed the dog to return from banishment, 'So long as you sit quietly.'

The animal settled on Adam's feet, and he felt a sudden rush of affection. It was nice to be liked.

'You didn't come to see me to ask after the dog, did you?'

She shook her head. 'I wanted to ask about your gallery owner. And...' she paused, as if hesitant to go on. 'I need your advice.'

She picked up her bag, and pulled out one of her textbooks. It flipped open and she took out a scrap of paper. Adam glanced over her shoulder at the list of scribbled plant names. They meant nothing to him.

'These are some of the flowers I saw in the painting. They're rare – and stolen.'

Another long pause. He waited until she took a deep breath and finished in a rush of words.

'I think my father might have been involved in the thefts.'

Adam took a moment to think. He'd expected her to talk about her husband. Instead, she seemed obsessed with her father and these plants. Was that because the subject of Greg's death was too painful, or was there another reason?

'Go on,' he said.

'I've seen some of the hotel accounts. The place is in debt. I think my father used hotel funds to buy illegal plants.' She told him how she'd tracked down the orchid and water lily. 'They shouldn't be in my father's possession at all.' She held out the list. 'Can you find out more? Like,' she seemed to find it hard to continue, 'did my father have stolen property, or maybe Daniel just added the flowers into the painting?'

Adam took the list, leaned back and closed his eyes, thinking.

Daniel. She'd mentioned him before, and there was an odd, self-conscious look on her face when she said the name.

'Tell me more about Daniel,' he asked. 'Did you have a relationship?'

Her eyebrows shot up. 'I suppose I should expect that from a detective,' she snapped, her eyes flashing. 'It's not really any of your business.'

'Ex-detective,' Adam corrected her. 'And it's not my business, but you asked for my help. Please, don't take me for a fool.'

She looked down, examining her fingernails. 'I suppose you think I might have been having a secret affair with Daniel, and that's why I killed my husband.'

'That's a leap.' Adam almost laughed. 'Not everyone who has an affair is a murderer, and I know better than to make assumptions without evidence.'

'Well, I wasn't. I told you, I haven't seen or heard from Daniel for years.' She was blushing.

Adam folded her list and tucked it in his pocket. 'Very well, I'll look into the plant thefts, if you like, but since we're being honest with each other, I think you should know the police think Greg was poisoned.'

She gasped, suddenly pale. 'I thought it was an accident, or suicide...'

'Did you?' Adam looked into her face, trying to read her emotions, watching for – what? Horror? Guilt? 'If I were working on your case, we wouldn't be having this conversation. I'm in a privileged position, with no responsibility for solving the murder. Still, I'm curious.'

She chewed on her lower lip. 'I don't know what I can say.'

Another silence stretched out until Adam was sure she had nothing else to offer. At least she wasn't coming up with bluster or bluff, alibis or theories, or accusations against anyone else. He really couldn't see her as a ruthless killer.

He said, 'Let's consider the facts. You invited me into your garden, where we discovered the body. It hadn't been there long. The location must have been part of a plan, but whether it was your plan, or someone else's, I can't know.'

Imogen's face remained impassive, so he moved on.

'You had a quarrel with your husband.'

She made a tiny noise.

He shot a sharp look at her face. 'Did you tell the police about it?'

She fiddled with the hem of her jumper, not meeting his eye.

'Right, I'll take that for a no. That could be a big mistake. As soon as the police find out, and they will, you'll look guilty.'

'And they already think I did it?'

'You're the most obvious suspect.'

'So, what can I do?'

Adam considered, and finally, with a feeling of burning his boats, he said, 'We'll find the murderer ourselves. Which means you have to be completely honest with me.'

Her face lit up. 'You'll help?'

'Why not? It was my job for years.'

'You're not like most police officers.'

'Because I'm not tall enough?'

She had the grace to blush. 'I didn't mean that.'

'Come on, now, what did I just say? You have to tell the truth. Anyway, Hercule Poirot was short and he was a detective.'

'Hercule Poirot was fictional.'

'Good point,' he acknowledged.

'It's not about height, or being tough,' Imogen said, slowly. 'I think it's because you're so cheerful. You smile a lot, and everyone likes you. All the hotel staff say you've cheered the village since you arrived. Mrs Topsham positively drooled when I mentioned you in the shop.'

Adam took off his spectacles and polished them vigorously, suddenly hot with embarrassment. He spoke slowly, 'I've learned, over a lifetime, to look on the bright side. I'm short and fat, I can't see beyond the end of my nose, and I'm going bald. I'm not clever, or funny, but I'm an optimist. My glass stays half full. I believe, against all the odds, that my toast will usually land butter side up.'

Imogen sat in silence. 'I wish...'

'You wish you felt that way?'

She nodded.

'Keep working at it, that's my advice.'

Mentally he added, *I have to.*

'Now,' said Adam, to turn the conversation away from himself. 'We have two mysteries here. One is your husband's probable murder and the other, your father's possibly shady business with plants, which involves this Daniel from your past. Let's put that to one side for a moment.' He went on, 'I'll trace Greg's movements since the two of you parted company. Where do you think he went? Who would he visit?'

She tapped the spoon on the back of her right hand.

Left-handed, Adam noted. Not that it made any difference.

'Actually,' she confessed, 'about a month ago, he got back in touch with me, saying he'd made a mistake and he wanted to see me. He said he'd broken up with the woman, whoever she was, and realised he missed me.'

Adam prompted, 'And you said...?'

She looked up and laughed. 'I told him I never wanted to see him or hear from him again, and left. I may have raised my voice a little.' She dropped the spoon back into the saucer and leaned back, eyes glinting. 'It was one of my finest moments. If he thought I would let him come crawling back after that, he was crazy. I was glad to see the back of him.' She gave a short laugh. 'But if that doesn't make me sound like I wanted to kill him; I can't imagine what would.'

'How did he contact you?' Adam asked. 'Did he come to your flat?'

'No chance of that, I'd changed the locks the day after he left. He rang and I agreed to meet him in a coffee shop.'

'I'll ask you to write down the date and the details in a minute, but first, tell me more. How was he? Pleading, sad, confident?'

Another pause.

'It sounds daft, but the word I'd use to describe him was shifty. He wouldn't tell me where he'd been living, or if he was with friends. I suppose he thought I might make a fuss.'

'Would you have done that?'

She grinned. 'Possibly, if I'm honest. All he'd say was that he thought he'd had a bit of a midlife crisis, and he was over it, and he'd like to come back, please. Actually, I decided he was just missing a decent meal. He liked to be looked after, did Greg.'

Adam rubbed his chin with his knuckles. 'Not too much to go on, but give me the date and place you met and I'll visit, see if anyone remembers your meeting. Not,' he added, 'that it points to innocence or guilt, but there may be something useful. Anyway, it's a start. Any objections?'

She shrugged. 'None at all.'

'And while you're giving me addresses, make a note of anyone you think Greg may have visited after your break-up.'

13

Imogen met Emily halfway up the stairs. 'We are totally full to bursting,' the manager enthused. 'The phones have hardly stopped ringing, and I've had to put Alex on to full-time email duty.' Alex was Emily's assistant.

'Well, they say no publicity is bad publicity,' said Imogen. 'By the way, I shall be out most of today and tomorrow. Are we properly staffed to keep things going?'

'Definitely. I've done a list of everything that's going on in the hotel, so you don't need to worry at all. It's all in hand.'

Imogen resisted the temptation to nitpick as she ran her finger down the lists of room occupation, taxis, meals, and workmen. She couldn't fault Emily's efficiency, but she wasn't happy. Did Emily know the hotel was in trouble, and if so, why hadn't she mentioned it? 'Have you got a minute?' She led the way into the small office behind reception where the two could sit perched on hard chairs, elbows leaning against a pair of wooden desks.

Emily's desk was covered in neat piles of paperwork, each held down by a Caithness paperweight.

Imogen sat at the spare desk, wishing she felt less like an interloper and more like the owner.

'Emily, you worked with my father for two years, so you must have known a good deal about his business.'

Emily blushed bright red. Her eyes flickered round the room, looking anywhere except for Imogen's face. 'Well, I only really knew about the hotel. The councillor had other businesses that were nothing to do with me.'

Imogen persisted. 'But I'm sure you took phone calls and saw emails that were sent to the hotel?'

Emily cleared her throat. 'There were plenty of communications. The staff dealt with anything they could, and if they were unsure, they would print out emails and give them to me. I'd check them over for hotel business and send them to the councillor if they were... more private.'

Imogen leaned forward. 'I'm sure you behaved impeccably. Unfortunately, the hotel's not as profitable as it should be. I've looked through my father's papers. I'm concerned at the year-on-year losses, despite healthy revenue. We need to consider our costs.'

Emily blinked, as though Imogen's grasp of the business surprised her. She sat a little straighter.

Imogen continued, 'I'd like you to go through the accounts for discrepancies. I shall do the same. I've already printed out all the information we have for the past five years, but I'll let you make your own copies.'

And that will stop you fiddling the books. If that's what you've been doing.

* * *

Imogen made her way up to her own small suite of bedroom, bathroom, sitting room and office, to change into gardening clothes. The sun had come out, and perhaps the garden was dry enough for her to trim back overgrown hedges and pull a few weeds from the borders.

Outside, she found Oswald, her father's long-serving gardener, far away from the orangery, clearing brambles. Oswald had worked at the hotel since Imogen was a child, a source of warmth, company, and a hot cup of tea when Imogen found life with her father too difficult to manage.

'Miss Imogen.'

The familiar Somerset burr was music to Imogen's ears. Hot tears rose to her eyes.

'I'm so sorry I haven't seen you since father's funeral. The flowers you arranged were perfect. Thank you. I should have told you before.'

'Now, don't you go worrying about that, Miss Imogen. You've had a lot on your hands, what with your husband's body and everything.' He raised his eyes to the heavens. 'That husband of yours, causing trouble.'

Imogen gasped. 'Really, Oswald.'

'I speak as I find, as you well know. I bet you rue the day you married that man.'

'It's not his fault someone killed him.'

'Had it coming, he did. Only a matter of time. Never trust a man who buys a leather jacket in middle age.'

Imogen had bought the jacket for Greg.

'Oswald, you're going to stay and help me with the garden, aren't you?'

The elderly man dug his fork into the ground and leaned on the handle. 'Well, miss, I thought you might not need me around now. What with you being a proper landscape gardener and all, I thought you'd bring in a new team.'

'Don't be ridiculous. I learned more from you than from any university course. Anyway, I'm going to be away at times, overseeing the work at Haselbury House, and I've got plans for this garden – I'll need your help with those.'

The old man's lips curled in a slow smile.

'For the moment, I wanted to ask you about the old days. Do you remember the painters who came to paint the garden? It was a good few years ago, when I was a teenager.'

'And I was a younger man, in those days. Married to Sylvia, with a couple of young ones driving us crazy, and no aches in my bones.'

'And how are your family?' She should have asked before.

'All quite well, miss, although Sylvia's getting on a bit. She's been nagging, lately, wanting me to work less and spend a bit more time at home. Especially now the boys have children of their own.'

'So you're a grandfather? How wonderful.' Imogen gulped. She had no children, so she'd never enjoy any visits from her own grandchildren.

'That's right. Noisy little blighters they are too, a couple of girls and a boy. They like to come and help in the garden from time to time, which I hope you won't mind, miss. That Emily doesn't like it, but the councillor never stopped me, so she has to put up with it.'

Imogen hid a grin of unworthy triumph. Emily's efficiency hadn't made her popular.

'Your grandchildren are more than welcome.'

He nodded in the measured way he did everything. 'You were asking, miss, about that time the artists came. That David, he spent weeks here.' He squinted, thinking. 'No, not David – Daniel, that was the name. You and he got on like a house on fire. Thought you might marry him.'

'I married Greg instead.' There was an edge to Imogen's voice. 'We were already engaged when Daniel came. Anyway, that wasn't what I wanted to talk about. He painted some plants that I can't find in the garden.' She tried to sound casual. 'Unusual flowers. Orchids, for one. I wondered about them. I mean, if we'd been growing rare orchids, we surely would have propagated them, grown more and sold them on.'

Oswald shifted from one leg to the other. 'Ah,' he said, and his mouth snapped shut.

'Come on, Oswald,' she coaxed. 'Nothing happened in this garden without your knowledge. Were you growing rare plants?'

The old man narrowed his eyes, brushed a lump of mud from the shaft of his spade, and looked away towards the stream. 'Well, it was like this. I didn't know how your father got hold of those plants. He liked unusual flowers, see. He brought them to me, from time to time, and I grew them on, in the orangery. At least, most of them – the tender ones. We had to boost the heating. Your dad told me they came from the tropics.' He took an enormous handkerchief from his pocket and mopped his face. There were beads of sweat on his neck. 'I was away, one day, showing some of the vegetables at the local show, and when I came back, your father had sold them on. A van had come to pick them up and that was the end of that.'

'You never grew them again?'

The old man rolled his head from side to side. 'Not so far as I know.'

That could mean anything. Imogen wondered if she was making too much of it. Keen gardeners often tried and failed to grow exotic specimens.

She left Oswald with his wheelbarrow and spent an hour

tidying, watching this year's blossom bursting into life among bright green foliage. On her knees, hands deep in the rich red soil, the smell of earth filling her nostrils, she managed to forget about her father and his suspect activities.

14

STEPH

Adam stared at the address of the cafe where Imogen had met with her husband: The Copper Kettle, Camilton. She'd added a mobile phone number and another address. 'I think Steph Aldred might be back in Camilton, or her parents, at least. This is their address. Greg and I knew Steph at school. I haven't seen her since, but Greg was often away on business…'

The Copper Kettle could wait until later. Adam wanted to know where the murder victim had lived after leaving his wife, and this was the only lead he had. Perhaps Steph might know.

He drew his car to a halt in a quiet street near the station. Stepping out, he leaned on the wall overlooking the railway lines, remembering how badly he'd wanted to become a train driver when he was five.

He snorted. There were lots of things he'd wanted when he was young. For one thing, he'd ached to grow as tall as his friends.

Adam tore himself away from the railway just as a train clattered through. He turned up a side road.

Number fifteen turned out to be a small, semi-detached

house with a neat garden and a gate that clicked cheerfully when he closed it. Somewhere, a piano played some kind of jazz or ragtime – Adam had no idea what it might be.

He rang the bell, the music stopped, and a short, dark-haired woman opened the door.

About the same age as Imogen, she wore joggers with a casual grey cable jumper. She had no make-up, but high cheekbones and large brown eyes.

'I'm hoping you know someone called Gregory Bishop.' Adam fidgeted slightly, uncomfortable. He missed his police badge and the right to ask personal questions.

The woman took a step back. 'I-I don't know him.'

'May I come in a moment?' Adam offered his warmest smile.

She licked her lips and looked Adam up and down. 'Who wants to know?'

'I'm a friend of Imogen Bishop – Imogen Jones, she used to be.'

She gave a little gasp. For a second, Adam feared she was about to shut the door in his face, but after a moment, she stood back and waved him through to a small, cheerfully furnished room. A bright Indian throw lay across the sofa. Scatter cushions in jewel colours decorated a pair of armchairs and an orange footstool stood near the fireplace.

The woman gestured vaguely at one of the chairs and sat on the sofa, gathering herself neatly together, with crossed legs and folded arms.

She would be giving nothing away if she could avoid it.

'I can see you know the names,' Adam said. 'Let's not play games.'

'I knew them a little, if that's what you mean. We were—' she stopped herself.

'You were friends in the past?' Adam suggested.

She nodded. 'Who are you?'

Adam opened his arms wide in a non-threatening gesture. 'My name's Adam Hennessy.

'Steph—' again she pulled herself up short, frowned for a second, appeared to decide she was no match for her visitor and said, the words tumbling together, 'I'm Steph Aldred. I haven't seen Greg for a long time, but I read in the paper that he died. I haven't seen Imogen for years.' She rubbed her nose. Was she telling the truth?

'It's not that he died, so much, as that he was murdered, and the police suspect Imogen.' Adam added, in a conversational tone, 'I take it you didn't murder him.'

The woman's hands flew to her cheeks. 'Of course not – why would you think – I never – I mean, I hardly know him these days.'

'These days?'

Another torrent of words. 'I knew him years ago, when we were at school, he wasn't in my school, of course, because it was girls only, but the boys' school was nearby. My parents could hardly afford the fees, but they were keen on a good education.'

Adam nodded solemnly, letting her talk.

'Greg was at the boys' school. They kept us all apart in those days, of course, but we were allowed to meet up for after-school activities.' She blushed. 'By after-school activities, I mean clubs and societies. Although, we did pair up from time to time. That's only natural, isn't it?'

Things, Adam reflected, were different in those days.

'I expect you mean dramatic societies and choirs, and such-like? We had similar activities when I was young.'

The woman's lips twitched. Was she struggling to imagine her visitor looking young?

Adam looked round the room, searching for signs of male

occupation, but saw nothing; no jacket slung carelessly over a chair, or games console.

Steph said, 'Greg and I were in a combined orchestra. I played the flute, not particularly well, and he played the trumpet. He was even worse.' She'd relaxed a little. 'Once, he played a different piece of music to everyone else. The conductor didn't even seem to notice. We were that bad.'

Adam's next question, 'When did you last see him?' wiped the smile off her face.

She rose and, agitated, walked round the room plumping cushions, moving ornaments, straightening a curtain.

Adam waited.

At last, she turned.

'He came here at the beginning of February; I think it was. He didn't stay long. Not overnight, or anything like that. He came because he was upset. He'd broken up with his wife, Imogen, and he wanted to talk about it.'

Steph's face softened at the memory. Adam wondered whether she was lonely. Perhaps that explained why she'd let him, a stranger, into her home so readily.

He took a chance with a personal question. 'Do you have a partner – a husband or something?'

She gave a little shake of her head. 'I'm divorced. I have a daughter, Rose, but she's away, at university. This place is a bit of an empty nest at the moment.'

Adam ignored the sympathy he felt. He was here to help Imogen. He knew better than to believe a witness, just because he found her attractive.

'Where did Greg go after he left you?'

'We talked about people he knew in the area. You see, this is a small city. Many live here all their lives. Only the brave ones go off to London after university. The rest of us like it here in Camilton. It's comfortable.'

'Quaint?'

She smiled. 'I suppose you could say that. We sound boring.'

'Not everyone stayed in the area, did they? Your friends, I mean.'

She stiffened. 'No. In any case, Greg didn't want to visit anyone else. He said he was too upset to tell the story again. I think,' she coloured, 'I think he was hoping I'd ask him to stay, but to be honest, I never really liked the man. Why Imogen married him, I've no idea. She could have chosen anyone.'

Adam got to his feet. 'You've been very helpful,' he said.

Steph leaned a hand on the door handle. 'I'm sorry Greg's dead. Even though I didn't like him much. I hope, you know, it wasn't too horrible. The papers didn't say...'

'A rather nasty dose of rat poison, I'm afraid.'

15

BIKE

Adam drove home, prepared for the dog's exuberance, relieved to find his furniture intact. 'You're learning,' he said, 'and it's time you had a name.' He lifted the dog's lead from a hook near the door. 'Tell you what, we'll walk through the village and name you after something we find.'

The two set off, and for once, the dog walked to heel.

A car sped through the village at top speed, skidding past The Plough, around the corner and out of sight. Adam listened for the crash.

Sure enough, a squeal of brakes told him the car had met an immovable object.

'Come on, dog.' Adam set off at a run, the animal loping alongside.

The car owner stood, arms akimbo, in the middle of the road.

Nearby, a bicycle lay on its side, wheels and handlebars askew, while its owner, a lad of about fourteen, struggled to heave it upright.

The car driver shouted, 'You could have been killed, you

idiot.' He pointed to a scratch leading from the front to the rear of the vehicle. 'And look what you've done to my car.'

Adam ignored him and ran past, to the boy's side, 'Are you hurt?'

The boy shook his head and sniffed. Adam peered into his face.

'Come into The Plough.' He pointed around the corner. 'We'll get you cleaned up and call someone to deal with your bike.' He turned his attention to the driver. 'Councillor Smith, isn't it? We'll need to call the police. The boy's nose is bleeding. Any crash that involves injury needs to be reported. I'll phone them, but you need to wait here until they arrive.'

The councillor muttered under his breath.

'What was that?' Adam asked, velvet covering steel in his voice.

'Glad the lad's all right,' the man grunted.

'So far as we can see.' Adam said. 'He needs checking out – a bloody nose means a bump on the head. Could be concussed.' Councillor Smith snorted.

Adam led the boy to The Plough and phoned the police.

The woman who took his call sounded uninterested, since no one was badly hurt, but agreed to 'send someone to check'.

The boy sat on the sofa, visibly struggling to hold back tears. The dog laid his head on the boy's knee, graciously allowing himself to be stroked, as Adam rang the local doctor and arranged for a paramedic from the surgery to look the boy over.

'My dad will go mad,' the boy sniffed. 'He told me not to ride round there. It's the hill, you see. You can get up a bit of speed going down. I didn't expect to meet anyone at the bottom, though.'

'No one ever does,' Adam remarked. 'Still, don't worry too

much about your dad. Councillor Smith was travelling too fast in that Mercedes of his, and I'm a witness. As is the dog, of course.'

The animal looked up, as if he knew Adam was talking about him.

'What's his name?' the boy asked.

'He doesn't have a name.'

'Why not?' His hands had stopped trembling.

'He recently arrived. No idea where he came from. No collar, no chip, nothing.'

'He's adopted you?'

'So it seems.'

The boy was smiling.

'What do you think we should call him?' Adam asked.

The boy's tongue poked out with concentration. 'Harley,' he said.

'Harley? Why would I call a dog Harley?'

'I'm gonna get a Harley in a couple of years' time. Harley-Davidson. It's a bike.'

'I know what a Harley-Davidson is, thank you.' Adam laughed. 'Hey, dog,' he called. 'What do you think of Harley as a name?'

The dog trotted over and jumped up, trying to lick Adam's face.

'You have to stop doing that, dog. Harley, I mean. Now,' he went on to the boy, 'I can hear a car arriving, and I expect it's the paramedic, to make sure you haven't done yourself any serious mischief. The one advantage of crashing into Councillor Smith's car is that the mention of his name gets local services rushing in circles. But you may want to stay out of his way for a while. Bikes aren't insured, so he'll have to use his own insurers to cover that rather ugly scratch on the side of his bodywork.'

The boy's face fell. 'I bet he'll go to our house telling my dad to pay up.'

'Leave that to me.' Adam still knew a thing or two about traffic police. He was pretty sure they'd put the fear of publicity into the councillor's head. 'We'll head the councillor off. But I'm afraid your bike is well and truly dead.'

* * *

The paramedic gave Alfie Croft, the young boy, a clean bill of health, pronounced a hospital visit unnecessary, and left. The nosebleed had almost dried up by now.

A couple of phone calls tracked down the boy's mother, at work in a supermarket in Camilton, and she soon arrived to take charge of her son.

'That Councillor Smith.' Disgust was written all over her face. 'Thinks he's above the law. Get away with anything, politicians do, what with their flashy cars and big houses. That Councillor Jones across the road, he's another one – rest his soul,' she added, flustered. 'Forgot he was dead, for a moment.'

'Did you know him?' Adam asked.

She snorted. 'Oh, everyone knew him. Thought himself Lord of the Manor, he did. Our Alfie, here, used to deliver papers to the hotel, back in the day before everyone read their news online. Never got no tips nor nothing at Christmas, nor any other time. Mean old so-and-so, that councillor. And what with all those young girls employed around the place, who knows what they were getting up to?'

'The staff, you mean?'

'I do. Always young – young enough to be his granddaughters, I reckon. Always female, and pretty. Most of them didn't stay long.

I reckon the man couldn't keep his hands to himself, that's what I reckon.'

Adam wondered if Imogen would recognise that description. Perhaps she would – that might explain her cool attitude to her father.

Alfie's mum was still talking. 'Talk about murders,' she went on, an excited gleam in her little round eyes, 'I wouldn't be surprised if the councillor had been buried in the garden, that I wouldn't. There's more than one person wanted to see the back of him, and that's a fact.'

Adam shot a glance at Alfie, relieved to see he was happily playing tug-of-war with Harley and the remains of one of Adam's slippers.

Seeing the boy was in no hurry to get home, Adam offered Mrs Croft a cup of coffee and a slice of cake.

'Why, don't mind if I do.' Her face lit up. 'Nothing nicer than a slice of cake and a nice cup of tea when you've had a bit of a shock, now is there?'

Adam bustled about in his little kitchen. He could hear the chef clattering in the pub kitchen, making last minute arrangements before the doors opened. As the tea brewed, Adam left his visitors and put his head round the door.

'Everything all right, Josh?'

The chef stirred with one hand and offered a thumbs up with the other. 'Hunky-dory,' he shouted.

Adam grinned. Josh was Australian, after all.

As Mrs Croft and Alfie tucked into enormous slices of chocolate cake, Adam wondered aloud why councillors behaved badly.

'I'm sure they don't start out that way,' he said, hoping his guest would take the hint and pass on more gossip about Councillor Jones and his colleagues.

Mrs Croft picked up the last few crumbs of cake and licked

her fingers with delicacy. She launched into a description of Councillor Jones' career in the hotel.

'And the way he treated that daughter of his, well, there's no excuse. Such a nice girl she was, the image of her mother, I'm told. He never forgave her for going off to study gardening and not taking over the hotel. Free labour, I suppose he wanted.'

Adam said, 'I've heard the councillor had his fingers in all the local pies, as well as the hotel?'

'You bet he did. Any scheme in the county, and he'd be there. How do you think he got planning permission for all the renovations to The Streamside, like that new spa at the back? Such a lovely quiet little hotel it was a few years ago, even though it was nothing like it should have been. The previous owner had seen to that.'

She wiped her mouth on a napkin. 'But the councillor, he could never stop adding bits here and walls there, and if you ask me, he ruined the place. My Fred,' Fred must be her husband, Alfie's dad. Adam wouldn't stop the flow of information to ask. 'My Fred said he should have been locked up long ago. There were plenty of folks put out when he opened that spa affair at the back of the hotel. Irene that owns the leisure centre in Camilton, for one. He ruined her business, he did. She and her husband had to close down.'

She paused, apparently running out of tittle-tattle. 'More cake?' Adam offered, in a ploy to keep her talking, but she heaved herself reluctantly to her feet.

'Better not, got to watch this tummy of mine.' She reverted to a stage whisper, as though sharing a shocking secret, 'Run to fat, you do, at my time of life.' She raised her voice, 'Come on now, Alfie. Leave that poor dog alone and we'll get home. And don't you worry about your dad,' Adam could hear her, still talking, as they left The Plough. 'I'll make it all right with him.'

Adam pondered the female staff at the hotel. Was there truth in any of Mrs Croft's allegations?

Josh unlocked the doors of The Plough, and the first customers ordered beer. Another opportunity, perhaps, to pick up a little gossip.

Adam joined the barman behind the bar.

16

RESTAURANT

A red jacket. That was what Imogen needed for the reunion. Not a red dress – that was far too obviously 'look at me', but a red jacket would lift her spirits, and she had just the thing. There was something about the clash of the jacket with her red hair that turned heads.

When had she last worn it?

She thought for a moment.

That was it – for the interview at Haselbury House.

She'd known that landscaping the gardens there would put her designs on the map. The house had a new owner, recently enriched through clever investment in buy-to-let properties, and even more recently ennobled with a title for services to charity. He planned to make this new home the envy of the county, and money was no object. Imogen couldn't let such a prize slip through her fingers.

Sure enough, the jacket had worked its magic. Martin Jenkins CBE had awarded her the contract on the spot.

She'd still been wearing the lucky jacket when she met Greg for a celebratory dinner that night.

They'd rolled home in a taxi, buoyed with excitement and champagne. She'd tossed the jacket into a bag of clothes that needed dry-cleaning.

The dry-cleaner nearest to the flat had closed, and rather than search farther afield, she'd stuffed the bag in a corner, only retrieving it when she moved back to the hotel.

It had lain, forgotten during the move, at the bottom of a wardrobe ever since then. It was going to be a crumpled mess.

She clicked her tongue as she rummaged around until she found a black plastic sack, squashed into a corner under a pile of woollen socks.

She pulled the crumpled jacket out and shook it. Could a spot of ironing do the trick?

She sniffed, smelt stale alcohol and abandoned the idea.

What a shame.

She smoothed down the velvet nap, the feel of it evoking that surge of excitement when Martin Jenkins shook her hand to seal the deal. Her fingers snagged on the edge of a pocket, where the stitching had given way. She investigated further and pulled out the bill from the restaurant.

She'd insisted on paying that night, and Greg had laughed. 'Now you're going to be rich, why not?'

She looked again at the total and shuddered. Georgiou's was easily the most expensive restaurant in town.

'Let's push the boat out for once,' Greg had said, when she'd suggested a smaller place. 'Don't be so stingy.'

Their meals outside the flat had always been low-key affairs, usually burgers at a fast food chain. Greg had often said he hated posh food – 'You get a square inch of meat and some fancy sauce. I like a proper man's meal.'

She'd had no idea he'd eaten at Georgiou's before.

She'd been even more surprised when he whispered behind his hand to the waiter.

'What did you say?'

He'd waved a hand in the air. 'I supplied Joe Georgiou with computer equipment. Did him a favour. Thought he'd like to come and say hello.' Greg had winked. 'Ah, here he comes.'

The restaurant owner, tall, with receding hair, wire-rimmed glasses, and an expensive looking suit, had scuttled across the floor.

'Gregory, my friend,' he'd gushed in a Mediterranean accent, rubbing his hands together. 'And this must be your lovely partner.'

'My wife. We're celebrating.'

'Excellent. I love a celebration. Is it a birthday?'

Imogen had opened her mouth to speak, but Greg had interrupted. 'She's a landscape architect and she's going to redesign the grounds at Haselbury House.'

Joe Georgiou had beamed, a line of sweat forming on his upper lip. 'Many congratulations, Mrs Bishop.' He'd clapped his hands, bringing the waitress skidding to their table. 'Two bottles of our best champagne for my friend Gregory and his wife. Be quick.'

He'd waved away Imogen's thanks, losing interest as his eyes followed the figure of the waitress as she hurried away.

Imogen had been glad when he left them to their meal. There had been a look exchanged between the two men that made her uncomfortable.

Greg enjoyed making deals, but he never discussed them with her, and she'd long stopped asking.

They'd both drunk far more than usual, that evening. She'd spilled half a glass of champagne on her best red jacket, giggling like a child, and Greg had phoned for a taxi to get them home.

Now, she held the bill in one hand, sat on the bed, and closed her eyes. That was the last time she and Greg had enjoyed each other's company. They'd led almost separate lives for years.

She needed to know more about Greg's activities. Had he been involved in shady deals, and could they have led to his death?

She ought to give Adam Hennessy the address of the restaurant.

Now, though, Imogen was off to a reunion, and if she couldn't wear the old, stained and crumpled red jacket, she'd make do with her cream silk blouse and tight-fitting black trousers.

She'd call on Adam tomorrow morning and tell him about Joe Georgiou.

17

Imogen drew up, stomach churning, at her old school, thirty year old memories whirling in her head.

Since the school closed, the building had become an entertainment venue.

It was smaller than she remembered. The track on her right had led to the hockey sheds, while the left-hand path headed to the sixth form entrance.

She steadied herself against the car, already regretting the four inch heels that pinched her toes. She checked the ballerinas in her bag. She'd be needing those soon.

'Imogen Jones.' Imogen gasped as Mrs Hall, biology and art, appeared, over seventy but still styling her hair in a neat grey roll around her head.

Imogen held out a hand, felt warm, dry fingers on hers, and a rush of déjà vu. The years dropped away and she was a tongue-tied schoolgirl again.

She struggled for words. 'How are you? You look so well. I mean, are you still...' She stumbled to a halt.

'You mean, fancy me still being alive, don't you, dear? Well, I'm happily retired and thrilled to be invited back here.' Her blue eyes, bright as ever, twinkled at Imogen. 'I'm in the reception party. Toni asked me to look out for you.' The smile faded. 'I'm so sorry to hear of your loss. Your father was a pillar of the community and a good friend to the school. We wanted to let you know how sad we all were to hear of his accident.'

'We?'

'Yes, some of the girls have been planning a reunion for your year group, but no one was sure how to get in touch with you. I had no idea you'd returned to the hotel until I read about your husband's death. You poor thing, you must be devastated.' She gave Imogen's arm a squeeze. 'But, then, Toni tells me she bumped into you anyway, in town. Wasn't that a happy coincidence?'

Imogen swallowed. No need to tell her teacher she'd been in the police station.

'Wasn't it,' she murmured, following Mrs Hall along the familiar path to the left.

The sixth form common room looked oddly familiar, yet different. Sleek leather sofas had replaced the ancient, worn-out chairs and the unwieldy piles of books, primarily used to hold coffee mugs, had disappeared.

Imogen could almost smell musty books and cheap perfume from the old days.

The hubbub in the room rose at each new arrival. Imogen scanned faces. Her old companions had aged, lines had popped up round eyes and mouths, but she would have known them anywhere.

Toni grabbed her, kissing both cheeks. 'How wonderful that you've come. I wasn't sure—'

'Nor was I, to be honest, but since you'd taken the trouble to invite me...'

Toni's laugh was high-pitched.

'Fancy us meeting in town like that. How do you like being back home?'

Home? The hotel felt nothing like home. 'It's... strange. My father's things are still there. I haven't finished going through them yet.'

As the awkward conversation with Toni stalled, Imogen heard her name bawled above the hubbub. Kate, her oldest and best friend, hardly changed at all, was waving like a maniac from the other side of the room.

Imogen waved back, her hand freezing mid-air as Kate's companion turned, glass of red wine in hand, and smiled. Imogen knew that lop-sided grin so well.

'Daniel?' Her heart thudded rhythmically. He looked exactly as he had when he came to paint the hotel garden so long ago.

Ignoring Toni's vocal admiration of her shoes, Imogen crossed the room, knowing the only reason she'd come to this excruciating event was the hope of seeing Daniel again.

* * *

Kate hugged Imogen. 'It's been so long. We need to catch up. I promised to take a glass of wine to Mrs Hall, so give me just one moment and I'll be back...'

She drifted away.

Daniel hadn't changed at all. Grey speckled his hair and lines radiated from his eyes, but the handsome man under those sharp cheekbones and wide mouth was exactly as she remembered.

'Imogen.' Daniel's brown eyes glowed. 'I'm so sorry about your father.'

'Thank you.'

'And your husband, too. You must be devastated.' A frown line surfaced above Daniel's eyes. 'Suddenly, you're on your own.'

Imogen had to swallow hard to keep tears from her eyes. Trust Daniel to understand.

'I wish I'd been a better daughter.'

The babble of conversation in the room died away as they talked. Familiar tunes played in the background, but Imogen could hardly hear them. Her world contained only Daniel.

In the days to come, she would remember so little of their conversation. It was nonsense, mostly; life's small successes and failures. They talked about Imogen's career, her big commission at the stately home and her love of getting her hands dirty.

Daniel talked about painting. He was poor but happy. He'd had some exhibitions, made enough to live on, married a French girl he'd met while studying in Paris. He had a son. 'Amelie and I drifted apart. She's still in France, in the south. Pierre lives with her and I visit when I can.'

As they talked, Imogen watched those familiar brown eyes, sure she was about to drown in them, wondering if this was the moment – that one, special moment – when her life would change, miraculously, and she would spend the rest of it in a glow of happiness.

Marriage, growing old together; the whole dream beckoned. It was late in life, but not too late. She felt young again, tonight, as though she'd only just left school.

Someone squeezed past and touched Daniel lightly on his back. 'Can I join you two if you're gossiping about old times?'

Daniel turned and pulled Imogen's old friend, Steph, close, his arm around her shoulders. 'We're just catching up on the news. We haven't even started on "do you remember" yet.'

Someone must have punched Imogen in the stomach, for suddenly she could hardly breathe. Daniel and Steph? Together? Look, he was smiling into her eyes...

With a shaky hand, Imogen raised her glass, gulping down wine, not tasting a drop. 'I see you two have kept in touch,' she managed.

Steph laughed. 'I bumped into Daniel last year.'

'I've been out of the loop.' Imogen spoke through numb lips, knowing she sounded distant. 'And I need to catch up with everyone.' Desperate to escape, she searched the crowd. 'Kate,' she gasped. 'There you are.' Her friend was still talking to Mrs Hall.

Without another glance at Daniel or Steph, fighting to maintain the few shreds of dignity that remained as her dream crashed at her feet, she lifted her chin and strode across the room. 'Thank heaven you're here.'

The two old friends hugged again; Imogen close to tears. At least she had the excuse of two recent bereavements. No one would be surprised if she were tearful. She wiped her eyes, blew her nose, and hugged Kate again.

'Why didn't we keep up with each other? It's been years. What have you been doing? Maths, that was your thing. Maths and art.'

'I trained as an architect. It took years.'

Imogen glanced at her friend's hand and Kate laughed.

'No, I never married. I'm a career girl.'

'Me too. I'm a landscape designer.'

'Really – we should work together.'

'We should.'

A brief silence took hold, the two women avoiding eye contact. They were both thinking the same thing. The elephant in the room loomed.

'We all lost touch, didn't we, after...' Kate's voice trailed away.

'After that horrible night.' Imogen grasped the nettle. 'You know, I was never sure exactly what happened.'

'Me neither. I mean, I remember us all scrambling down the tunnel, lighting candles and opening bottles of wine. I think I drank so much I passed out...'

'Me too.'

They stopped talking. Imogen tried to recall that night, as she had so many times over the years, but everything was blurry.

Kate broke the silence. 'The boys spiked the drinks.'

Imogen nodded. 'That was it. Everyone was high. We didn't know what was happening. One minute we were laughing and dancing, and the next, that fight broke out and we ran all the way back to the school.'

'Except for Julian.'

Imogen closed her eyes. 'Poor Julian. Concussion, they said. He fell against the wall when we all ran. Hit his head.'

'That's right, concussion.' Kate's face was pale.

Imogen murmured, under her breath, 'And now, Greg's dead.'

But it was Julian's face in her head. Small and skinny, the butt of people's jokes, tagging on to the popular lads who hung around Imogen's group. Well, hung around Toni, mostly. Julian had always been nearby, a bit of a swot, too earnest, a terrible dancer. He'd been tolerated, but no one had really cared if he'd been there or not.

Until, suddenly, he wasn't anywhere.

The boys had stopped hanging out with the girls, then. Everyone buried their heads in their books, pretending they had to work, had no time for parties.

Except for Greg. He'd called at the hotel one day, asked Imogen out to the pictures. It had been a relief to be with him. He was a joker. He made Imogen laugh, and that meant she never had to think about Julian, or how he'd asked her out that evening in the tunnel, or how she'd laughed at him and his big spectacles.

They never, in all the years they were married, referred to that night. Nor did they mention Julian. It was as though nothing had ever happened, and Julian had never existed.

Adam sat in the Copper Kettle, nursing a cup of coffee and munching on a slice of home-made fruit cake with appreciation. This tasted better than the average teashop fare. Over the years, he'd spent many hours in far less pleasant eating places, from greasy spoons and motorway service stations to backstreet pubs.

A quiet afternoon in a little coffee shop felt precious, despite the gingham tablecloths and ever-lasting – by which he meant plastic – flower arrangements. A couple of elderly ladies sipped from patterned china cups, pouring refills from surprisingly capacious teapots and nibbling at Victoria sponges.

Adam looked again at the address Imogen had scribbled. Sure enough, she'd met her husband here, for the last time. 'Odd,' Adam muttered under his breath. This wasn't at all the place he'd choose to host a showdown between a separated couple. For one thing, the acoustics were terrible. He could hear every word the ladies nearby uttered. In fact, much of his energy was spent trying to tune out the story of one lady's unfortunate contact with the local hospital.

'And I said to him, I've never been one for taking pills, but if you insist, I'll have a go. After all, I'm too old for it to matter much. Got to die of something, haven't we?' She cackled and took another bite of cake.

'My Edward died because of his heart,' her friend rejoined. 'Gave out, it did, one day. There he was, halfway up the ladder – and I told him he was too jolly old for climbing ladders, but did he take any notice of me? Did he ever...' She paused for a sip of tea. 'Now, where was I, dear?'

'He were up the ladder...'

'That's right, Joan. I was inside, making a cuppa, when I heard the crash. Shocking, it was, made me drop my cup. Fell right on the geraniums, he did, and he'd nurtured those plants.'

'Ladder wobbled, did it?'

'Don't really know what happened. Heart gave out, that's all I know. The doctors said it was shock, but whether his heart stopped and that's why he fell off the ladder, or whether it was the shock of the fall that did the trick, they couldn't tell.'

'An accident, then.'

'I'd told him.' She wagged a finger in the air. 'Accidents happen as you get older, and he should have known better. Silly old fool.' She sighed, 'I miss the old beggar, though. It's too quiet around the place on my own.'

Her friend sighed in sympathy. 'What you need is a cat,' she pronounced. 'Cats are company. And what's more, they don't answer back.'

The two friends chortled happily.

Adam shot them an admiring glance. Resilience, that's what those women had, in buckets.

That made him think of Imogen. She had a similar quality. Close family members dying all around, but she soldiered on alone. Always supposing, he remembered, she hadn't killed her husband. The lack of fuss half convinced Adam she was innocent.

A murderer would make sure to show considerably more distress. Imogen kept her emotions private.

Adam stopped eating. The elderly ladies had finished their tea and were gathering up handbags and shopping, ready to leave, but he no longer noticed. What was it they'd said? Accidents happen as you get older.

An accident.

The councilor, Imogen's father, had died in an accident.

Accidents happen all the time and no one had questioned that one.

Adam dragged his phone from a pocket and googled the newspaper reports of the councillor's crash. No other car had been involved. He'd been driving along the road when a tyre exploded. Apparently, the treads were old and worn, and one had picked up a nail from the side of the road. Police had examined the nail, for they found several nails and screws on the roadside, along with a couple of old planks. The road was notorious for fly-tipping; Adam had seen a pile of old mattresses more than once; fly-tipping in the countryside was a constant nuisance.

No witnesses, and the source of the planks and nails unknown. Not many clues there.

The councillor, the newspaper pointed out, had failed to take his car for its annual service for a couple of years. Worn tyres could be killers, the police emphasised, warning the public to take care.

Adam remained still for a long time, letting his coffee cool, wondering how many people knew the councillor never bothered to take his car for a service. The staff at the hotel, perhaps, and maybe his daughter.

Was it worth opening up a whole can of worms when chances were the accident was genuine?

Once a police officer... Adam picked up the phone again. He

wouldn't be able to rest without investigating, and he knew a man who might be able to help.

Once Adam had made the call and the ladies had left, he showed Gregory's and Imogen's photographs to the waitress. She'd been working that day but shook her head. 'We get all sorts in here. Can't remember them all. Don't have much of a memory for faces, I don't.'

'These two were quarrelling.'

She laughed. 'That happens all the time. Mind you, it's usually about the shopping. You know, how long it takes the wife to choose a dress and how bad-tempered the husband gets. Since I started work in the cafe, I stopped taking my old man shopping – it just leads to trouble.'

* * *

Adam drove home, his head full of exploding tyres. Those ladies had been worth their weight in gold – and it was a considerable weight. He wished he'd bought them more cake. His afternoon at the Copper Kettle had turned out to be a most useful hour or two.

He hummed along to Bonnie Tyler, breaking into loud, tune-less singing when Abba came on, singing 'Waterloo'. Pop music was his secret guilty pleasure.

He turned the corner to The Plough, his home. Who wouldn't want to live here, in this picture perfect village, surrounded by fields of blinding yellow rape, and young, green barley? The few neat houses seemed to doze, as though nothing could ever happen here, but human nature in the countryside could be as dishonest, violent and unpleasant as in any town. At least, in Lower Hembrow, there were plenty of folk as caring, warm and cheerful as Alfie's mum.

Just now, though, Adam needed to deal with Harley. The dog

had settled in happily enough at The Plough, but Adam had thought of a much better place for him. He hated leaving the animal at home, but he wasn't used to taking a dog everywhere he went. Harley needed a proper dog person.

As he slipped through the gate leading to his private entrance and unlocked the door, Adam heard the familiar clatter of Harley's toenails on the wood floors, followed by his ear-splitting howl. He pushed the door open and the dog leapt in the air, thrilled to have more human company.

Adam glanced beyond, to the trail of mild destruction that culminated in a heap of half-chewed slippers.

'That's it, Harley. You're a lovely fellow, but you need someone who understands your doggy ways. Tomorrow, we find you a new home.'

19

Imogen slept fitfully after the reunion. She'd drunk little more than that single glass of wine, but her head ached as though she'd emptied a bottle. Through the night, a series of dreams had shaken her awake, time and again, her pulse beating fast and her stomach churning.

The reunion had been even worse than she'd expected.

In her dreams, the pallid, bespectacled face of Julian had haunted her. How had she managed not to think about him for so long, as though he'd never existed?

She caught her breath. It was Toni's fault. She'd tracked Imogen down, purely to make sure she attended the reunion; she'd wanted to make trouble. That had always been Toni's role at school. She hadn't even been involved in the plans for the night picnic. She'd heard about it and forced herself on Imogen and her friends.

Imogen should have known better than listen to her when they met in the department store. Toni was untrustworthy, sneaking around, listening and watching, and using people for her own ends.

Then, there was Daniel. Reluctantly, Imogen tried to face facts. She'd been a fool to let her emotions run away with her, just as they had when he came to paint her father's garden. Daniel had thrown his arm around Steph, and she'd smiled into his eyes. They were an item, and Imogen must accept it and move on.

She caught sight of herself in her mirror and groaned. Her face was white, her hair stuck out like a holly bush, grey roots showing under the auburn, and her mascara had run under her eyes. What a sight.

She ran her hands through her hair to tame it. It was time to take control of her life.

Look at Adam Hennessy. He always had a smile on his face. Imogen would follow his example.

She'd start by solving Greg's murder. She had a lead, after all.

She'd left the restaurant bill from that miserable evening with Greg on her dressing table. She washed her face, scrabbled in her bedroom drawer, pulled out a lipstick and painted her mouth bright red. She dressed hurriedly, stuffed the bill in her pocket and drove to Georgiou's.

* * *

She hammered on the door. A short, weary looking youth with a sparse moustache mouthed at her through the glass, pointing at the sign on the door. The restaurant was closed. She hammered again, and he dragged the door open.

'I said, we're closed.' He carried a broom in one hand and wore a grubby apron.

'I'm here to speak to Joe Georgiou.'

The youth's eyes flickered from side to side, as though searching for help with this unreasonable woman. He looked nervous.

Imogen put on her most authoritative voice. 'Now, please.' She tapped her foot.

It was too much for the young man. He shouted over his shoulder, 'Uncle Joe. Someone to see you.'

His uncle hurried into the room. 'This is your last warning, Spiro. Only those with appointments come into my restaurant in the morning—' He broke off and looked Imogen up and down, eyes narrowing. 'I recognise you.' He frowned. 'I never forget a face, although hundreds come to this, the premier dining venue in town.' He smoothed his moustache, a far more luxurious affair his nephew's. 'I have it. You are the wife of my late friend, Gregory. Mrs Bishop,' he almost bowed. 'I am so sorry to hear about his death, and that of your dear father. I would have come to the funeral myself, but, alas, there was an important function in this very restaurant at the same time. A gathering of producers and actors, discussing a forthcoming Netflix series of mysteries. You would have recognised some of them – Sam Henderson, the producer? The actor, Ron Wolf?'

Imogen shrugged and his face fell. He reeled off the names of a few more minor celebrities.

'Mr Georgiou,' Imogen interrupted. 'I'm here to find out why my husband was such a good friend of yours.'

'Gregory and I had a friendly business relationship.' He shifted from one foot to the other. 'He supplied me with computer equipment.'

'At a special price?'

He jabbed a finger in her direction. 'I'm not about to discuss commercial matters with you.'

She changed tack. 'How did you know my father?'

He threw his arms wide. 'We were in the Rotary Club together. Two successful local businessmen. That cannot be a surprise?'

'No, I suppose not,' she admitted. What had she hoped to achieve by coming here? Had she imagined this arrogant businessman was going to describe his deals? Especially if the deals were less than honest.

She would learn nothing from him.

She let Joe Georgiou take her hand in a brief, clammy handshake, and left.

* * *

An hour later, she jogged alongside Adam Hennessy as he followed the stray dog, now named Harley, through the village.

'Sorry about this,' Adam panted, 'but this animal has far too much energy. I can't keep up with him, and he's wrecking my home. He chewed my best shoes while I was away yesterday.'

'You could keep him away from your things.'

Adam stopped. 'You've seen the size of my place. There's just no room for him.'

She laughed. 'The Plough's plenty big enough.'

The dog made a lunge forward, possibly having caught sight of a rabbit in the hedgerow, almost pulling Adam off his feet.

'But, I'm not, and Harley needs true love.'

Imogen laughed aloud. 'I knew you'd cheer me up.'

'I'm glad my misfortune makes you happy.' Adam's sideways smile took the sting from his words. 'But, seriously, this dog is too much for me. I need to make The Plough pay, and constant dog walking and furniture replacement takes far too much time. I should be ordering supplies right now, but here I am, scampering along behind this crazy animal. I'll go bankrupt if this goes on. A police pension has its limits.' He coughed, 'In fact,' he sounded uncertain, 'I'm planning to send Harley to the animal shelter. I hear there's a great one not far away. He's a nice dog, and given a bit of discipline, he'll be a good pet. I just don't have the time or energy to train him.'

Imogen stopped in her tracks, hands on her hips. 'You're joking, aren't you? Every pub should have a dog.'

'Not this one.' Adam hauled on the lead and pulled Harley back. 'Sit down,' he admonished. The dog ignored him.

Imogen raised her hand. 'Sit!' she commanded, and Harley sank back, tongue hanging out, panting expectantly. 'Have you got a treat for him?'

Adam delved into one of the pockets of his jacket. 'Dog biscuits.' He handed one to Imogen, who held it aloft.

The dog's eyes followed every move she made, until she announced, 'There you are,' and tossed it towards the animal. He caught and swallowed it in one bite. 'You just have to use clear commands.'

'I can see you know dogs,' Adam threw her a sideways glance.

'I grew up with them. Labradors, mostly, and once, a red setter.' She took the lead from Adam's hand. 'Now, heel,' she said, and Harley trotted beside her, so close he was almost touching her legs. 'He's been trained,' she pointed out.

'Still, he's got to go. I've made up my mind.'

Imogen took a long moment to reply. 'You know, he loved running in the hotel grounds. Maybe...'

'He did. Perfect exercise, I'd say. Just right for an animal like this.'

Encouraged, Imogen said, 'Maybe he'd like to stay with me for a bit. If you really don't want him. And if we can't find his owner.'

'Seriously? You mean, you'd take him off my hands?'

'If you can bear to part with him.' She bent down. 'You're lovely, aren't you, Harley?'

Adam beamed. 'You'll be doing me the most enormous favour. I'll never be able to repay you. Ask me for anything.'

Imogen stood tall. 'Find my husband's killer.'

* * *

Within half an hour, Adam and Imogen had collected all Harley's doggy possessions from The Plough. 'It's tidier already.' He ignored the pang of regret, handed over Harley's lead and followed Imogen and her new companion across the road to The Streamside Hotel.

'Let's take him straight out into the garden,' Imogen suggested. 'I'll explain to Emily and the others later that he's here to stay. I'm sure they'll be delighted.'

'I hope you're right.' He wasn't so sure.

He followed her along the path they'd taken on the night of Greg's death, towards the orangery.

She stopped. 'I'm not quite ready to go inside yet,'

'Give yourself time.'

'I might have to knock it down; replace it with a grove of trees.'

'Like those?' Adam pointed at the hawthorns lining the bank of the stream. 'They're magnificent.'

'There's a bench nearby– let's sit there a moment while Harley chases imaginary rabbits.'

They sat facing the stream where a family of ducks paddled serenely.

Imogen said, 'I meant it – about finding Greg's killer.'

'I'll do my best.

He thought hard, filling the pause by pulling out his notebook and making a show of finding the right page.

How sure was he of Imogen's innocence? Was he being

trapped by friendship into ignoring facts?

Speaking with care, he described his visit to Steph Aldred.

Imogen's head jerked up at the name.

'I saw her, too, at the reunion,' she said.

'Well, she didn't have much to tell me. Your husband visited her after your quarrel, looking for somewhere to stay, but she refused him and he left. She said she didn't know where he went.'

Imogen's hands had stilled. 'Was she living alone?' she blurted, and a blush rose to her cheeks.

'So far as I could see. She told me she was divorced and her daughter had left home. How about you? You were going to find Daniel.'

The blush grew deeper. Jealousy?

Adam waited for Imogen to speak.

'He was at our school reunion. So was Steph, and my best friend from school, Kate. We talked a lot about the old days.'

'Reminiscences not entirely happy?'

Imogen's words came in a rush. 'It reminded me of something dreadful that happened just before we left school.'

Words tumbling over each other, she told the story of the picnic in the tunnel that ended in disaster, and the death of the unfortunate, unloved Julian.

'We all laughed at him because he was different. Too clever, hopeless at sport and not at all attractive.'

Adam swallowed. She could have been describing him and his schooldays, always on the outside of every group.

'I was the worst.' She twisted her fingers together and heaved a huge sigh. 'He asked me to go to the pictures with him, and I laughed at him.'

Adam nodded. 'Teenagers are cruel animals. Most of us improve as we grow up. You'd be kinder, now, and Julian would have found his own tribe – people who value him as he deserved.

That's the biggest tragedy of an early death. Julian never had the chance to become his real self.'

Gaze still on her hands, she nodded. 'You're right. He was a good person, and clever. He'd been accepted by one of the Oxford colleges. But we didn't really notice him, because we only cared about good looks, and being trendy, and so on.' She gave an awkward smile. 'Do people even say "trendy" these days?'

Adam flipped to a clean page in his notebook and cleared his throat. 'Tell me more about him.'

'Why?' Imogen looked startled. 'He doesn't have anything to do with Greg's death. Greg was there that night, we all were, but none of us saw Julian get hurt. We found out later that he tripped and hit his head against the wall. It was just a freak accident – we were all either drunk or high. It could have happened to any of us.'

'Are you sure?'

Imogen's mouth fell open.

Before she could speak, Maria Rostropova's voice cut through the tension. 'My darlings. I've tracked you down. Your receptionist said you would be out here, Mrs Bishop, with my dear friend, Adam, so I took the liberty of coming to find you.'

'You're very welcome,' Imogen said, 'though I don't think we've met...?'

'My darling, I came to your dear father's funeral, although I could only stay for a few moments. He and I were great friends. The best of friends.'

'Thank you,'

Maria was still talking. 'If he had still been here, he would have loved to help me with my concert.' She peered into Imogen's face. 'Has Adam not told you about the concert?'

'Seems to have slipped my mind,' Adam said. He'd been trying not to think about it, regretting his promise almost as soon as he'd made it. He really shouldn't let Maria twist him around her little finger.

He explained their arrangement to Imogen. 'I'm hoping it's all organised?' He shot a look at Maria, already anticipating the answer.

She threw both her hands in the air. 'Organised? Why, I was leaving all that to you – you promised.'

'I'm sure I didn't—' He broke off and started again. 'Maria,' he said, 'I'm happy for you to organise your charity concert in my garden—'

'Your musical space.'

'Quite. However, I need you to do the work. Do you understand? You must organise rehearsals, tickets, volunteers to manage the event...'

'Me?' Maria was shocked. 'I have no idea how to find tickets, or who will volunteer. Remember, I am just a poor—'

'Yes, a poor, immigrant widow. You told me.'

Adam felt completely out of his depth with this beautiful woman.

To his amazement, Imogen stepped in. 'Emily, my hotel manager, is the most efficient person on the planet. I'll ask her to help out.'

Maria Rostropova's eyes shone with triumph as Adam suppressed the urge to laugh out loud. It seemed it was Imogen's turn to fall straight into the woman's trap.

Hands clasped as though she were in heaven, Maria sashayed elegantly over to the stream, turned and swept one arm wide, taking in the whole of the garden. 'And these wonderful grounds...'

'No,' Adam said. 'You cannot force Mrs Bishop to hold the event here.'

'But I'd be delighted.' Adam stared. Was she mad?

'Do you have a date in mind?' Imogen went on.

'Three weeks. We plan to perform in just three weeks' time. We have been rehearsing for months.' Maria raised a pencilled eyebrow at Adam. 'You see, I have already arranged all our rehearsals with our conductor. I am not so silly as you think, dear Adam.'

As she drifted away, Adam rolled his eyes at Imogen. 'And that,' he said, 'is manipulation at its finest.'

'Thanks, mate.' James took a long, hard pull at his pint. 'This is on the house, right? Sorry I couldn't talk when you rang. I was inside a drunk's chest at the time. What can I do for you? You need my brains?'

Adam rested an elbow on the bar of The Plough. 'Thanks for pulling strings. The local DCI called round to tell me he's pretty sure Greg Bishop was poisoned.'

'A pleasure. And what else can I do for you in return for more free beer?'

'I need some DIY knowledge.'

James glanced round, sucking in his cheeks. 'Making a few changes?'

'Not me. I'm about as handy with a hammer as a snake with a spade. I like this place just as it is, and if I need to change things, I'll get a builder in. No, it's more forensic...'

'Got a body handy?'

'No, just a set of tyres with nails.'

'You dinged your car?'

Adam recounted Councillor Jones' crash and the pile of

rubbish that caused it. 'The police took a quick look and wrote to the man's daughter, saying there were no witnesses, and nothing suspicious, so they were closing the case.'

'And you disagree. Wait a moment,' James held out a hand, one finger raised. 'I'm trying to connect the dots here. I thought you were investigating your girlfriend's husband's murder.'

'Not a girlfriend – just a friend. And yes, I am. I'm also curious about her father's death.'

'Oh, ho. Now you're talking,' James crowed. 'A double murder sounds juicy. What can I do to help? The body's buried, I suppose. Are you going for a exhumation, because if you are—'

'Nothing like that. It was definitely a car crash, and probably not murder at all.'

James gave a snort of derision.

Adam ignored it. 'I went to the scrap yard and retrieved the nails from the tyres. I need to know if we can trace them – if there's anything unusual. You're a DIY freak. Can you give me an idea what they might be used for? It's a very long shot, but worth a try. I hoped you'd have a contact.'

'Not wanting to involve your old team?'

'That's right.' Adam hated the idea of his former colleagues knowing he was dabbling in amateur sleuthing. He could imagine their comments. 'And definitely not the local police. They're not keen on talking to me.'

'Scared of your reputation, I bet. The great Adam Hennessy, best clear-up stats in the region, put the biggest criminals behind bars—'

The biggest of them all, the killer of Adam's cat, was in prison swearing vengeance. 'I think I cramp their style. So, can you help?'

'Show me.'

Adam pulled a plastic bag out of his pocket. Inside were three nails, each very different from the others.

James poked them. 'You didn't take these from an evidence bag?'

'Don't worry. The police didn't want them. There's no evidence chain.'

James finished his pint and pushed the glass across the bar. 'While I'm working on it...'

'You're going to drink me dry.'

'That's the plan.'

James laid the nails on the bar in a neat row, while Adam served a local young farmer getting a round in. He glanced at James; his brow was furrowed in concentration.

Adam washed glasses and waited.

It was early evening, and apart from the young farmers, the place was empty. A few bookings for food would be in later, and it was Wednesday, so there would be a few midweek walk-ins. He'd be rushed off his feet by the end of the night.

He shot a glance at the healthy young farmers. The sleeves of their shirts, rolled above their elbows, looked in imminent danger of splitting, straining to cover muscles developed far from any gym. The country life looked pretty good. What could beat serving behind his own bar?

James looked up.

'What do you reckon these are for, then?' Adam asked.

'You remember when the wife insisted on a potting shed?'

'You mean, when you wanted a place away from the kids.'

'Who wouldn't? My idea of gardening – a couple of chairs and a cupboard for whisky. Anyway, we went the whole hog, got the builders in and had a permanent structure. Needed planning permission and all sorts, but Pam handled all that side of it. Bear with me, I'm telling you this because of the roof. Proper slate.

Going to outlast me, that's for sure. Anyway, this stainless-steel affair,' he held up a long piece of metal with an L-shaped hook at one end, 'is a slate hook. And this,' he pointed to a nail that gleamed with a copper glow, 'this one's called a clout nail, and again, it's used in roofing.'

Adam leaned across the bar and clapped his friend on the shoulder. 'You're a genius. Anything about the other nail?'

James rolled a finger across the third item. 'It's a screw, not a nail, my ignorant friend. It's big enough for a roof, but not necessarily. These others, though, they're more conclusive.' He went on in a fake French accent. 'My little grey cells tell me the fly-tipped pile of rubbish was either from a slate roof – unlikely, as there were no slates mentioned in the reports – or it was left by a builder – or, more specifically, a roofer.'

'Thank you, Hercule.' Adam peered more closely at the three bits of metal. 'Not sure where that takes us, but it's good to know.'

James reverted to half cockney and waved his glass in Adam's face. 'All that deduction's thirsty work. Keep setting them up, my good man.'

* * *

As the pub filled, Adam kept the drink flowing.

Alison, the lively university student who waitressed in the evenings, scampered round, drawing appreciative stares from the regulars as she served.

'Over here, when you're ready.' The imperious voice booming from the end of the bar belonged to Jonathan Hampton. His family had owned the manor estate, where the hotel and pub were situated, before running out of money and selling it all off. Jonathan lived in London but made regular trips to stay at the hotel and visit The Plough – 'Need to make sure the place is doing us proud.'

'What can I get you?' Adam stuck to extreme politeness. The other man ordered a Manhattan cocktail for his girlfriend, a leggy blonde with a jarring accent and expensive handbag. James shifted a few inches along to make room for her at the bar.

Alison, four plates of steak and scampi balanced on her arms, winked at Adam as she swept past. He kept a straight face and concentrated on perfecting the cocktail and drawing a pint of best real ale.

'I hear the body in the Streamside garden was a murder.' Jonathan licked his lips. 'Bet it's brought in a few punters.'

A wizened farmer nearby chuckled. 'Plenty of drama here-abouts. And they say nothing ever happens here in Somerset.'

'Then, there's the councillor,' Jonathan continued at full volume. 'Knew him well, of course. Thinking of getting into politics myself.'

His girlfriend nodded, silently draining her glass and replacing it on the bar.

'One more,' Jonathan held up the empty glass. 'Got to keep the missus happy, eh. Oh, forgot, you don't have one of those. Lucky man.'

Maria Rostropova made an entrance, but Hampton was too busy chortling to notice until she tapped him on the shoulder.

'Slumming, Jonathan?' she smiled, a malicious glint in her eyes.

Jonathan, apparently impervious to irony, proudly introduced her to his girlfriend, Cecilia.

'And you are?' Maria turned the full force of her huge eyes on James.

'One of Adam's old mates. James.'

'Ah. From his work?'

'Not really. But I'm afraid my own work awaits.' James raised an appreciative eyebrow at Adam, jingled the metal roof fastenings in his pockets, and left.

Adam served a couple of new arrivals and turned back, as Maria said, 'The councillor was helping to fund our concert, but sadly, since he passed away, we're dreadfully short of funds. We're asking everyone to help out.'

The blatant plea for money reached into even Jonathan Hampton's thick head, and the man had the grace to blush. 'Don't get down here too often, I'm afraid. Not sure I can help.'

'But your company? I hear you're one of those successful bankers...'

The man's blush deepened, and he blustered, 'Maybe, some of our charity funds might be available...'

'Perhaps you have a business card?'

'Not on me, I'm afraid. Sorry.' He made a show of consulting his watch, a probably fake, Rolex. 'Good lord, is that the time? Come on, Cecilia, we'll be late for dinner. With the Smiths.'

A bark of cruel laughter followed the pair as they left. 'Good on yer, Mrs Rosti,' the farmer crowed. 'Don't have two pennies to rub together, he don't. Works in some tin-pot motor sales company.'

'Oh, I do hope I didn't embarrass the poor man.' Maria's smile was smug.

Adam plunged glasses into soapy water. 'You're shameless.'

She barely heard, for she was surrounded by awed locals promising to attend her concert and fighting to outdo each other with offers of help.

* * *

DCI Andrews kept Adam and James waiting for half an hour,

next morning, before seeing them. His face was a picture of disbelief, eyebrows rising and falling together and, at times, in opposition to each other. 'Are you trying to tell me the councillor's death was murder?'

Adam exchanged a resigned grimace with James. This meeting was going to be difficult.

'We've no real proof, but the signs point that way,' Adam began. 'There's the coincidence of Gregory Bishop's body turning up on the day of the councillor's funeral, in the councillor's garden.'

The detective chief inspector grunted. 'The killer could just have been taking advantage of the kerfuffle around the funeral.'

'True, or maybe he's trying to make the wife look guilty.'

'Well, that's not hard. She's at the top of my list. Still, go on. What else have the two of you discovered during your little piece of sleuthing?'

James took a deep breath.

Adam hurried to head off the imminent explosion. 'According to gossip in the village—'

Andrews interrupted, his voice heavy with sarcasm, 'I'm afraid local grapevine evidence is inadmissible in court.'

Adam held on to his temper. 'Of course, I know that, but it can sometimes point us in the right direction.'

Andrews gave a heavy sigh. 'Very well, what do the good people of Lower Hembrow say?'

'There's talk about the councillor's businesses. Folks wonder how he got planning permission for the hotel spa, for example – maybe he was on the take, or one of his friends was?'

'Skullduggery within the local council.' Andrews scoffed. He turned to James. 'What about you, Doctor? Anything to add? Made any deductions?' Antagonism fizzed between the two men.

James tossed the roof fastenings on the table. 'The debris that caused the accident came from a newly demolished roof. An old roof. These fastenings aren't made any more. Wherever they came from, it was built no later than the mid twentieth century.'

'And knocked down to make way for some of these thousands of new homes being built?'

'True,' Adam said, 'it's a long shot. But it's another lead, Detective Chief Inspector, even if not a great one.'

The police officer fingered the metal fastenings. 'These are no use as evidence, either. They could have been touched by the world and his wife. I can't make any kind of a case out of these.' He tossed them to Adam. 'I'm not convinced, yet, and I'm not about to offend the mayor and the town council by putting in a report that someone killed Councillor Jones, based on some rusty old nails and gossip about planning permission.' He glared at Adam. 'If you want to waste your time on demolished old buildings, be my guest.'

Harley careered round the hotel garden, stopping to sniff at every hedge and marking the occasional tree with his own scent. Imogen's face glowed with pleasure. Her cheeks were a healthy pink, whether from the walk or from excitement, Adam could not tell.

His plan had worked perfectly. If ever he'd met a woman in need of a dog, Imogen Bishop was that woman.

He'd miss Harley. The Plough seemed oddly quiet in the mornings, before the hurley-burley of a busy working day began, but a dog had been one responsibility too many.

'I don't want to waste your time,' she said, 'but I'm at my wit's end with finding Greg's killer. I've discovered that investigation isn't as easy as I expected. I went to visit one of Greg's contacts, but I got nowhere with him; in fact, he showed me the door. I didn't know what to ask.' She bit her lip. 'I know you're busy...'

'No more than you, with a hotel to run,' he pointed out.

'I have plenty of staff.'

Adam broke into laughter, and after a moment, Imogen joined in.

'Sorry, that sounds so grand,' she spluttered.

'I can't think of a better way of spending my time than solving a murder,' Adam remarked. 'So, while Harley destroys your grounds, let's sit down and run through our progress so far.'

Imogen led the way to a bench overlooking the stream.

Adam cleared his throat and bought time, pulling out his battered notebook and searching pockets for a pen.

Time for the conversation he was dreading. 'You told me Julian died, that evening at school. His death bothers me.'

She flinched, as though surprised. 'You and me, both. It was a terrible thing to happen, but what does it have to do with Greg?

'Indulge me for a moment. You never know what connection one thing may have to another – even after thirty years.'

She pushed her hair back from her face, still frowning. 'Greg was killed because of his shady business deals, I'm sure of it. Honestly, Adam, you should see that restaurant owner, Georgiou. He gave me the creeps.' She shivered at the memory. 'I bet he's involved.'

Adam took a deep breath. 'There's something I haven't told you. Something I haven't proved, yet, but my gut feeling tells me I'm right. If I am, Greg's death is not the only one we need to look at. We can't ignore Julian's, either.' He paused, watching her face. 'And then, there's the other death.'

Imogen's face drained of colour. 'What – what on earth do you mean. The other death? Who else died? I mean—'

Her eyes darkened as realisation dawned. 'Not, not my father? No.'

She rose from the bench and took a stumbling step backwards. 'That's nonsense. You're making it up. Dad's death was an accident.'

Adam waited for her to calm down and slide back onto the bench.

It was the first time he'd heard her call her father 'Dad'. That was good. It showed there was affection there, despite the years of bitterness towards her father.

While she sat frowning as though collecting her thoughts, Adam reflected on her behaviour. She hadn't tried to prove an alibi for herself. She'd told him the truth about her break-up with Greg, even though she'd lied about it at the police station, and she'd readily admitted she didn't get on with her father. Small things, perhaps, but those contradictions weren't the work of a cunning, cold-blooded murderer.

And now, the shock, horror and affection in her voice as she spoke about her father were, Adam was sure, completely genuine.

Relief flooded through him, along with a stab of anxiety. He might be sure she was innocent, but DCI Andrews was unlikely to see such tenuous indicators in the same light.

He said, 'Let's look at the circumstances of your father's death. It happened so close to Greg's murder that I couldn't ignore it, even though it seemed totally accidental. But, two members of your family dying within weeks of each other? That's a big coincidence. It kept nagging at me, so I asked my mate, James – he's a forensic pathologist – for his opinion.

He agrees the car accident could easily have been faked. That road's out of town, with no cameras on the stretch where the accident happened. Nails in the tyre – we've all picked one up at some time, but there were three in your father's wheel, from fly-tipping near the road. Just for a moment, take a leap of imagination. What if your father's death was deliberately set up? It opens up a whole new area of investigation.'

She remained on the bench, but her hands were clenched. She spoke slowly, with care. 'If you're right, there must be a reason – a motive. Who would want my father dead? Well, the police would say I did, of course. I inherited the hotel.'

'True, but let's put that aside for the moment.' He was blunt. 'I'm sorry, but your father may have been murdered, and we have to wonder whether there are other deaths to be taken into consideration.'

There was a very long pause before Imogen spoke. When she did, her hands were at her face, muffling her speech so that Adam had to listen hard.

'You mean Julian's death,' she whispered. 'You think Julian and my father were both murdered.' She shook her head so vigorously that strands of hair escaped from behind her ears and fell over her eyes. 'No. No. I can't believe it. They were both accidents. Dad was a rubbish driver, and he should have given up his licence long ago. And Julian – we were just teenagers, playing around with drugs and drinking too much. No one would kill Julian. Why would they want to?' She raised her head. 'Those were my friends at the picnic in the tunnel. None of them would dream of killing anyone.'

'That's what people always think. It's like finding out your next door neighbour murdered his wife. You say, "They were a lovely family. Nice and friendly – he'd say good morning every day." Yet, the friendly neighbour bullies his wife, and one day he loses his temper and hits her with a hammer.'

Imogen's shoulders gave a convulsive shiver and Adam fell silent. Had he gone too far?

He spoke more gently, 'Any sudden death is suspicious until proved otherwise.'

She nodded, eyes narrowed, thinking. Finally, she struck her fist on the bench. 'We have to know – I have to know. It sounds crazy – unbelievable – but you're a professional. I trust you. If you think they're all connected, then we must prove it, one way or the other.' Her eyes shone with purpose. 'What's more, if there really is a link, it must have something to do with my school friends. If someone I know killed my father and my husband, I mean to find out who it is.'

Everyone at the reunion was now under suspicion. Imogen tried to digest that fact as Adam questioned her in detail about the evening. Old addresses and new names – he listed them all in his notebook.

The stream of questions continued, until Imogen's head ached.

'Finally, I need to know more about Daniel,' Adam said, and her throat tightened.

She breathed slowly, in and out, fighting a wave of nausea. Not Daniel. Anyone but him.

Adam's voice went on, reasonable and calm. 'We need to look at everyone connected with the three of them – Greg, Julian and your father. We have to eliminate them all. Don't forget Daniel spent time at the hotel and he painted those rare plants.'

At that moment, Harley bounded up carrying an ancient tennis ball in his mouth, and dropped it with a wet squelch on Imogen's lap.

'He already knows he belongs with you,' Adam remarked.

Imogen kept her hand on the dog as she talked about Daniel, soothed by the warmth of the animal's body. 'Since we're being honest about everything,' she knew there was an edge to her voice, but she ploughed on, 'I've talked to the gardener about the rare plants and he remembers them. The reason I'm telling you is...' She stopped.

'Because you think your father's shady schemes might supply a motive for murder.'

The look on Adam's face sent a shiver up Imogen's spine.

'I want you to be very careful. Until we know why these three people died, you have to watch your step.'

Adam drove to Ford, Daniel's tiny village just outside Crewkerne, revelling in the June sunshine. The rain had kept away recently, and the sun shone bravely overhead, promising to grow even stronger. The trees had freshened up beautifully, with that brightest of greens seen only in the first half of the year.

Adam ran through his suspicions. He was sure his instincts were good, although the police might disagree. Linking the three deaths was a stretch, but his gut told him not to ignore the possibility.

It was just as well he enjoyed a challenge. There were lines of enquiry spreading in all directions, and he could hardly tell which were separate, and which lay in a tangled knot with the killer at its heart, pulling the strings like a puppeteer.

Adam changed gear and swung around a corner, wondering about Imogen's school friends. Were they just a bunch of thoughtless teenagers whose stupid prank ended in a death? They'd separated after Julian's death and kept away from Lower Hembrow for years, only to meet up just as the councillor and

Greg were killed. The timing shrieked design, but who had set up the reunion, and why?

Perhaps Daniel, whom Adam was about to meet, could shed a little light on them.

Adam turned on the radio, finding a cheerful tum-te-tum Andre Rieu waltz on Classic FM, and hummed along, out of tune, as he wound his way through pretty Somerset villages.

The sign for Ford appeared, half hidden by branches. Adam screeched to a halt and turned down a twisting, muddy track. It narrowed as it descended, until hedges on either side scraped the sides of the car. Just as it seemed the track would go nowhere, it turned sharp right, ending abruptly at a long, low barn conversion surrounded by a network of paddocks.

A pair of donkeys, sunning themselves in the paddock, treated Adam to an ear-splitting braying contest.

The barn door opened, and a man appeared: tall, dark and handsome, dressed in jeans and a cable jumper and carrying a bucket of feed for the donkeys. He turned and waved. So, this was Daniel. Adam disliked the man on sight. Too handsome and too confident for Adam's liking. He was also responsible for Imogen's broken heart, all those years ago, if Adam had read her blushes correctly when Daniel's name came up.

'I'll just give these to the creatures, or they'll make that noise for hours. Here, boys.' Daniel emptied the bucket into a trough, patting the animals' necks. 'Here's your lunch. Enjoy.' He wiped his hands on the back of his jeans before offering one to Adam. 'Mr Hennessy. Or should I say, Detective Chief Inspector?'

Adam sighed. The man had googled him after their brief phone call. It ruined his disguise. He'd been posing as a potential buyer of Daniel's work. So much for subterfuge.

'Nice place.' He nodded at the barn.

'Still a work in progress.'

'Are you doing it up yourself?'

'All the bits I can. I draw the line at electrics, but I can saw a plank of wood and hammer in a nail or two with the best of them.' He waved for Adam to follow and led the way to a door at the end of the barn. It opened into a wide room with a glass roof. 'My studio,' he announced.

Adam grinned. 'Plenty of northern light.'

Daniel raised an eyebrow. 'Are you a painter too?'

'Strictly amateur. A hobby.'

'And you have other hobbies? Like sleuthing?' Daniel gave a short laugh. 'Such an odd word, don't you think, sleuthing?'

'I call it investigation.'

The man infuriated Adam. Jealousy, he supposed. Some people had every advantage. Imogen's face changed whenever he mentioned Daniel's name. She glowed from within, a sure and totally unconscious sign of her true feelings.

Adam told himself gilded men like Daniel had problems, too. He tried to keep an open mind, but that first spurt of visceral dislike still kicked in. This man had better not hurt Imogen again.

Something in the sidelong look Daniel threw his way told Adam the negative vibes were mutual.

'I bought one of your paintings,' he said.

'Did you? Now, that's something I always like to hear. Where did you find it?'

Adam named the gallery. He didn't tell the artist his painting was sold as part of a job lot, to clear space. He wasn't that cruel.

'And, what did you think of it?' Less sure of himself, Daniel busied his hands putting mugs on a tray and feeding capsules into a coffee maker.

'It's good, but I'm more interested in the subject. The Stream-side Hotel.'

Daniel's hands stilled for a moment. He shot a quick look at

Adam's face before resuming coffee preparations. 'You know the hotel?'

'I own the pub across the street.'

Daniel laughed aloud. 'Whoever thought to build a pub right across from a hotel?'

'You'd be surprised. The two work together well. Hotel visitors come to the pub for an evening of local colour. In fact, the two buildings used to be part of the same estate.'

'So, you know the hotel owner?'

Adam smiled at the undercurrents swirling around. 'Both the previous owner, and the current one. And I believe you know the family well; from schooldays and painting the hotel garden?'

Daniel took his time sliding a mug of coffee across the central table, avoiding splodges of paint, jugs crammed with dozens of brushes, and heaps of paper. The table, like the whole room, was surprisingly neat and tidy.

Daniel had an organised mind. Judging by the man's pursed lips, it seemed it was working hard.

'Well, what is it you want to know, exactly?' Daniel settled in a chair; long legs stretched out.

The manufactured calm didn't fool Adam.

'I'm happy to show you my work,' Daniel went on, 'but let's not pretend you're here to admire the paintings, Inspector.' Barely veiled hostility grated in his voice.

Adam kept his notebook in his pocket, pushed his spectacles an inch further up his nose, ducked his head and spread his hands in the age-old gesture designed to show he had no weapon. 'On the contrary, one of your paintings intrigues me; a water-colour of the hotel garden. You did a good job. I love your vivid colours, but the work struck me as unfinished...'

A brief smile lit Daniel's face. 'It was my first commission. The councillor contacted me when I graduated from St Martin's—'

'The art school?'

Daniel nodded; eyes bright with pride. St Martin's was a respected school of Art, now known as Central St Martin's. He cleared his throat. 'Councillor Jones asked me to paint the hotel grounds. He wanted to display the work on the walls of the building, but—' He broke off.

Adam waited, but Daniel had fallen silent. Something to pick up later.

'I was wondering whether you had any sketches or photos you used for the painting?' he asked, in the meantime.

Daniel frowned. 'I make dozens of quick sketches. They help with the final painting. Like many landscape artists, I don't paint exactly what I see.'

'A mixture of reality and fantasy? I noticed the painting is almost impressionist in style.'

Daniel grinned. 'Except, of course, true impressionists work fast and directly, aiming to put the essence of a scene on the canvas, like Monet's famous haystack paintings. He tried to catch the light as it changed over time.' His enthusiasm overflowed. 'If you're interested, I'll show you some of the preliminary drawings.'

He leapt up and opened one of a set of narrow drawers in a nearby chest. He'd labelled each drawer neatly, with the place and date. He tugged out a file, dropped it on the table and slid out a handful of drawings, fanning them out on the table in front of Adam.

'See, here's a sketch of the garden, with all the different areas. Then, here are a couple that focus on a single area. Then these,' he shuffled a few single sheets to the top of the spread, 'these are individual plants. Here's a peony and a rose, and a couple of irises. Very satisfactory to paint, irises. Are you interested in botany, Inspector?' There was a hint of amusement in his eyes as he sat down.

'Not really. At least, not unless it's linked to crime.'

A muscle in Daniel's jaw twitched. 'I'm sorry?'

Adam, pleased at the effect of his surprise attack, abandoned the 'eager customer' pretence – he'd been rumbled before he arrived, anyway. He leaned forward until his face was close to the other man's. 'Why did you stop your work at the hotel? Are commissions so easy to come by that you could afford to abandon one half finished?'

Daniel swallowed. 'No, of course not. That job meant a great deal to me, but…' He looked away, avoiding Adam's eyes.

Adam waited.

At last, Daniel took a long breath. 'There was something going on at the hotel. You see, some plants are so rare and difficult to grow that they fetch enormous amounts of money. They're restricted – they only grow in certain conditions. Collectors pay thousands – tens of thousands – of pounds, to get their hands on these rarities. They don't care whether the plants are obtained legally or not.'

Adam nodded, as though hearing this for the first time, and pulled out his notebook and pen. 'And you discovered…?'

The other man grunted. 'Councillor Jones took me for a fool. You see that orangery?' He pointed to one of his sketches. 'That's where he kept his most precious plants.' He hesitated. 'Oswald, his gardener, kept them alive and propagated them. I don't think he had anything to do with smuggling them in, but I reckon the councillor was in it up to his neck.'

Adam wrote fast in his notebook. The orangery, where Greg was found. Was that significant?

Daniel's words tumbled over each other. He looked relieved to be telling someone the story. 'I made a stupid mistake.' He grimaced. 'I got talking to Oswald and he showed me what he called "the specials" at the back of the orangery, told me how rare they were. I sketched them and put them in the picture, thinking the councillor would be pleased.'

His laugh was bitter. 'The innocence of youth. I've learned over the years, Inspector, that a man who gives you a commission knows what he wants, and doesn't need a rooky straight from college making additions to the picture.' He smiled. 'In short, he threw me out. He didn't tell me why, and I left at once. I needed to get as far away as possible. I was mortified. I'd boasted to all my friends about this wonderful commission, and I'd fallen flat on my face.'

He gave a short laugh. 'My youthful ego couldn't cope with the shame. I moved to the Lake District to start again on my own. The councillor kept the painting, paying me a fraction of what it was worth.'

'He can't have hated it that much.'

Daniel chuckled. 'Councillor Jones didn't like to waste money.'

Adam considered. 'I suppose he hung on to it until he'd sold the stolen plants on, made a profit and turned his attention to other ways of making money.'

'I was proud of it, though – still am, to tell the truth. It was pretty good work. A bit derivative, but not bad as an apprentice piece.' Daniel chuckled. 'At least I still have the sketches – he didn't know about those. Once I calmed down, I wondered why he'd lost his cool over a picture. I started to ponder why, if he'd lost interest in the project, he kept the painting. That's when I looked a bit closer at the sketches. I did a little research, found the names of the plants, and realised what was going on.'

'But you didn't go to the police?'

'I should have, I know, but Jones was Imogen's father. I couldn't do that to her. I'd known her for years, at school and—' Again, that sharp cut-off, as though he'd said too much.

'While you were painting the hotel garden?'

'We grew close, but she was already engaged to Greg Bishop.' He almost spat the name. 'He was a bigger loser, even, than I was, but he'd seen her first. I hadn't spoken to her much when we were at school. Actually,' he gave a glimmer of a smile, 'I was a bit scared of her. She was very dignified. Tall and quiet, cleverer than me. She didn't chatter and giggle like some of the other girls. I could never think what to say when she was around, so I kept out of her way.'

Adam recognised the feeling; most teenage boys found girls terrifying.

'I found it easier to talk while I was painting. She was... well, lovely. She seemed to like me, too. If she hadn't been with Greg, maybe we'd have got together. Who knows where that might have led?' He looked into the distance; the sharp angles of his cheekbones softened. 'What a missed opportunity. Her dad sacked me, and I was too mortified to hang around. I just packed up and left without saying goodbye. I mean, it wasn't as though we'd been an item, or anything...'

'You'd made no promises.' Adam heard the sarcastic edge in his own voice, but Daniel just shrugged.

'That's right.' He bundled the sketches together. 'Immature doesn't begin to describe me, does it?' He paused, looking from the drawings to Adam. 'You didn't tell me why you're so interested?'

Adam chose his words with care. 'Imogen Bishop is a friend. As you know, she's taken a couple of hard knocks lately – her father dying, and then her husband. I'm looking into her husband's death.'

'Are you, now? Not leaving it to the police?'

'Maybe I can move things on a little faster.'

Daniel dropped the bundle of sketches on the table. 'You think I had something to do with it? That's why you turned up here. Jealousy of Imogen's husband as a motive for murder.' His eyes flashed. 'Seriously? You think I'd kill her husband in the hope of winning her, after all these years? That's just daft.

Anyway,' his fist banged the table, 'I didn't need to kill Greg because they'd already split up.'

'I'm not accusing you of anything, Mr Freeman. As I said on the phone, I saw your painting and I was curious about the plants. Imogen recognised them.'

Daniel grunted. 'Well, if you're so interested, you can borrow these, but I'll want them back. And, for the record,' his voice rose again as he shot a glance at Adam's notebook, 'I had nothing to do with any shady business the councillor might have been involved with. I was an innocent lad, trying to make a living out of art.'

'You've succeeded. You're selling pictures.'

'You looked me up?' A hint of pride.

Adam inclined his head. 'Of course.'

'I keep my head above water. I'm no genius, but I sell to rich London bankers who want landscapes full of picturesque trees, painted with exactly the right colours to set off the carpets in their oversized houses. Fortunately for my sanity, and my bank balance, I never tire of laying paint on canvas.'

Adam took the drawings. 'And, I'm a retired policeman wishing I had your talent.'

At the door, he turned. 'Don't fret about the plant business. It's a minor affair, and in the past. The councillor's not around to answer for his, shall we say, misdemeanours. No need to drag his reputation into the mud.' *Unless strictly necessary*, he added silently, recognising that both of them wanted to protect Imogen. 'By the way, were you part of that unfortunate picnic in the tunnel that ended with the death of one of your schoolmates?'

'You've heard about that, have you? It was a dreadful business. I was there, I'm sorry to say. We were all thoughtless idiots and Julian paid the price. You know the saddest part?'

'No. Enlighten me.'

'None of us really cared about Julian. We only worried about whether we'd get into trouble.' He laughed, harshly. 'You have every right to be disgusted.'

Adam spoke with care. 'You didn't keep in touch with anyone from those days?'

Daniel took his time to reply. 'Mrs Hall kept in touch. She was one of the teachers – well, my art teacher, as a matter of fact. She turned up at one of my exhibitions. I think she organised the reunion.'

COFFEE MORNING

'So pleased you could make it.' Helen Pickles ushered Imogen through the vicarage door. 'No Harley?'

'He can't be trusted around food, yet.'

'You could say the same for me.' At Helen's deep, throaty chuckle, the locals in her room looked up. 'Now, who do you know?'

The first gathering of local people since Imogen had returned to the village; she'd been tempted to send her apologies. Helen had arrived at the hotel one morning in Imogen's absence, and left a note inviting her to meet 'a few friends for coffee – strictly nothing religious'.

Was she ready for the scrutiny of the locals?

Don't be such a coward, she'd told herself. *You survived that dreadful reunion.*

Stitching a cheerful smile on her face, she accepted coffee and cake, and tried to remember names.

Mrs Croft – Barbara, that was her first name. Adam had mentioned her. Alfie, her son, had fallen from his bike.

'Sit beside me, dear,' Barbara grinned. 'It's so nice to have a new face in the village. I live up the lane, the other side of the church. Do you by any chance ring bells?'

'Sorry, no.'

'Oh.' Barbara's face fell. 'It's so hard to find ringers. We have to use Alfie sometimes, and he's hopeless – can't seem to count.'

'Bless his cotton socks.' That was Jenny Trevillian, the farmer's wife. 'They grow up far too fast, you know. Before you can blink, he'll have left home.' She focused on Imogen. 'How many do you have, Imogen?'

'Children? None.' She stopped a breath away from an apology.

'Ah, shame. I have six,' Jenny said. 'Would have gone for more, but,' she dropped her voice to a stage whisper, 'I had a bit of trouble with the last one – got stuck...'

Helen cleared her throat and bustled across to refill Imogen's cup. 'I don't know how you manage,' she told Jenny. 'You put us all to shame.'

Satisfied, the farmer's wife changed the subject. 'I'll bring you a few eggs, Imogen. All our hens are laying at the same time and I can't keep track of them. Free range, you see, leave their eggs everywhere. Our Jack Russell, Bob, he'll crawl into the hayrick and back out, holding an egg in his mouth, gentle as anything. Who would have believed it? Never breaks a single one.' She rocked with laughter, tears squeezing onto her cheeks.

Edwina Topsham, from the village shop, rolled her eyes. 'Now, then, Jenny, stop touting for business for five minutes. I want to know more about our new neighbour. What do you do when you're not running your lovely hotel?'

Imogen smiled, took a scone and cut it in half. 'I'm a gardener. I'm currently landscaping the gardens at Haselbury House.'

Barbara Croft said, 'I wish I had green fingers. I kill everything I touch.'

An awkward silence filled the room.

'No, no, I mean in the garden...'

Helen smoothed over the moment. 'Since I have you captive here, Imogen, can you tell me when to prune my clematis? I've looked it up, and all the books talk about Type One or Two or Three, and tell me to prune them in different months, until my head spins.'

'I'm afraid it depends on the clematis. Maybe I could come over and take a look one day?' Imogen suggested.

In the hubbub of bids for her advice, Imogen ladled cream on the cut sides of her scone and heaped jam on top.

Edwina chortled. 'Knew you were one of us. Jam on top every time. Good to have you in Lower Hembrow.' What had pleased Edwina Topsham most – free gardening advice or the way she ate a cream tea?

Jenny objected. 'Jam first, every time – that's how the Queen does it.'

In the fierce ensuing argument, Helen sat beside Imogen and murmured, 'Everyone wanted so much to meet you. We're going to miss your father, here. He was quite a celebrity in South Somerset.'

'Really? Because he was a councillor?'

'Oh, my goodness, much more than that.' She raised her voice. 'Edwina, Imogen doesn't know about the time the shop almost closed.'

'Your father didn't tell you? Well,' Edwina settled herself more comfortably on the vicar's sofa. 'It's hard to keep a shop going in a village like this, especially now people read their newspapers online, or get their news from the telly. We were almost broke when your father stepped in. Started fundraising, pulled in enough to set the shop up as a... Now, what do they call it, Barbara?'

'A community enterprise.'

'That's right – can't get my old tongue around the words. Still, that's what he did, and put a big wedge of his own money in the fund.'

Jenny Trevillion added, 'And then there was the village hall. Falling down, it was, and nowhere for the teenagers to go, to keep them out of mischief, until the councillor rounded up a few of his mates in the building trade. Pulled down the place and rebuilt it for a song. Quite an asset to the village, was Councillor Jones.'

Barbara Croft's mouth was pursed, as though she was eating a lime. 'Hmm.' She muttered, 'Time I was off. Plenty to do. Nice to meet you.' She sounded lukewarm.

The vicar whispered in Imogen's ear, 'Can't please everyone. She had a run-in with your dad over planning permission for the hotel spa. Don't let her bother you. Your father talked about you all the time. She's a little jealous, I think.'

Afterwards, Imogen strolled back to the hotel, puzzling over the mystery that was her father. Who was he: saviour of the village community or greedy fat cat? Saint or villain?

A weight settled in her chest. It was too late now. She'd never know the real Horace Jones.

There was Kate, at the entrance to Sheppy's Cider Museum, looking at her watch.

Imogen waved, 'Sorry I'm late. I was at a coffee morning.'

'A coffee morning? You? Who would have thought it? But you were always late.'

'Was I?' They hugged and Imogen, breathless, laughed. 'I think I've been inducted into the village grapevine, now.' She took a long look at her friend. 'I'm glad you texted. I meant to get your number at the reunion, but...'

'You left early. We hardly had time to talk. Was something wrong?'

'No, not really. It was just – seeing everyone brought that evening back – you know, the picnic in the tunnel. I'm still trying to decide whether meeting again was a good thing or not.'

Kate heaved an explosive sigh. 'I thought we should have some time together, away from everyone else. To talk about old times.'

They paid their entrance fee and strolled through the museum. Within minutes, they were giggling like schoolgirls.

'Do you remember,' Kate said, 'when Steph brought a pint of cider into school and we drank it in the Common Room...'

'And Mrs Hall arrived just as we finished. We'd probably have been expelled if she'd seen what we were doing.'

'You think she didn't know?' Kate snorted. 'She knew everything we did. She'd been the sixth form tutor for years. After all, it was only a pint...'

'And there were four of us. We weren't exactly drunk, were we?'

'She gave me a right telling-off when she caught me smoking behind the hockey shed.'

'I think she was more worried that you were with one of the boys.'

Lost in their reminiscences and catching up with their current lives – the hotel, Harley, Kate's work as an architect – they wandered round the museum, barely glancing at the seed drills, ploughs and other farm implements on display.

'Don't you just love the smell of cider apples?' Kate asked.

A louder voice interrupted. One of the attendants was talking to the desultory collection of visitors on this quiet morning. 'Legend has it, cider makers throw a dead rat in the mix. It's not true, of course. At least, not here. I can't vouch for other companies.'

'Who were you with, anyway, behind the sheds?' Imogen asked, lazily eyeing her friend. 'I don't think you ever confessed.'

Kate's face crumpled into a fit of mirth. 'Why, it was David.'

Imogen's happy mood turned. She shivered, as though a dark cloud had crossed the sun. 'Julian's friend?'

'It was nothing. He wanted an invitation to our adventure.'

'Did he? He tagged along with Julian, didn't he?' Maybe Kate was right. 'I wondered why they came.'

Kate wriggled. 'I didn't exactly suggest it, but you know how it was. He said Julian was dying to get off with you.'

'He asked me out,' Imogen confessed. 'I wasn't exactly kind to him.'

'That's how we were in those days.' Kate put a comforting hand through Imogen's arm. 'So wrapped up in our own feelings, we couldn't think about anyone else.'

'Did the police talk to you about that night?'

Kate nodded. 'They already knew most of the story by the time they came to our house. My mother insisted on staying in the room. Boy, was I in trouble? I told her I didn't take any drugs deliberately and someone had doctored the drinks, but you know what she was like...'

Imogen remembered a big boned, deep voiced Amazon of a woman.

Kate confessed, 'I was grounded for the rest of the term.'

'Me too.' Imogen's father been furious. Imogen had let him down, ruined his reputation. She shied away from the memory of his words – '*Your mother would be ashamed.*' Imogen thrust the ugly memory to the back of her mind. 'Did you know who spiked the drinks?'

'Well, yes.' Kate looked at her friend, eyes wide. 'I thought you knew. It was Daniel.'

A tremor swept through Imogen's body. Daniel? Was he really to blame? And, if he spiked the drinks, did he also... She could hardly bear to finish the thought.

'Are you all right?' Kate asked. 'You're looking a bit sick.'

'I'm fine. How do you know it was Daniel?'

'Don't you remember? We took the food. I brought sausage rolls, you pinched smoked salmon from your dad's hotel, I remember, very posh for those days. The boys brought the alcohol. Daniel poured the cider.'

Imogen remembered. 'I couldn't get my hands on the hotel champagne.'

The little procession had sneaked into school after dark through the window in the common room, in search of the legendary ghosts. They'd wedged the window handle so carefully with plasticine that it looked secure, but only a single shove pushed the window open. One of the boys hitched Steph, the smallest of the party, on their shoulders and she'd slipped inside to open the door. Stifling giggles, the party had ventured downstairs to the forbidden basement and tugged open the door that led to the underground passageway.

Imogen had stumbled against one of the boxes stored there, scraping her calf, letting out a yelp of pain.

'Shh!' the others had hissed.

'Sorry,' she'd whispered.

Waving torches, they'd walked on, the tunnel leading steadily upwards. Daniel was leading the way, flanked by Greg and Steph. 'You know, I think it's a dead end.' He'd stopped, focusing his torch along the wall in front.

The friends had run their fingers over the wall.

'It's bricked up,' Steph had grumbled.

Disappointed, the teenagers had thumped the bricks, trying to budge them, until they'd tested every inch.

'It's no good,' Greg had said, startling Imogen. He'd walked so quietly she'd had no idea he was nearby.

The light from her torch had swept over his grinning, excited face. Imogen had returned the smile, surprised at the little catch in her throat. Greg seemed very handsome that night.

'It looks like the route to the hill is blocked,' he'd said. 'Good job we have supplies. Let's have a drink.'

They'd settled, muttering that they'd always known there was no way through.

That was when the drinking had begun. They'd lit candles that hardly flickered in the still air, switched off the torches, and sat companionably on rugs. Imogen's head was soon swimming. Greg and Daniel had moved between them, topping up plastic cups. Kate, always organised, had vetoed glasses as too dangerous for a picnic in the dark.

Suddenly, Julian had appeared at Imogen's side. 'Imogen,' he'd begun, a trace of a stammer in his voice. '*Fatal Attraction*'s on at the pictures. D'you fancy coming?'

Imogen had laughed in his face.

Thinking about it now, she closed her eyes in pain, but she couldn't banish his face from her mind. He'd looked so earnest, so resigned.

'Nah. Not my sort of thing,' she'd said, not caring that he'd turned away. From the corner of her eye, she'd watched Daniel approaching with a bottle in each hand.

To her chagrin, he'd handed one to Greg and moved on. He hadn't seemed to notice her at all.

Soon, Imogen was leaning back against the wall, her eyes half closed. Everything after that was a blur. They must have repacked the boxes and carried everything back to the common room, but she had no memory of it.

Greg had walked home with her, both staggering and giggling, and grabbing each other to keep from falling over. 'See you tomorrow?' he'd said, and she'd nodded, in a dream.

It was not until the next morning that anyone had noticed Julian was missing.

26

PHONE CALL

Adam called at the hotel. 'I saw your friend, Daniel, at his new place. You were right about that plant scam.'

She'd hoped she was wrong.

Butterflies fluttered nervously in her stomach.

'Is it far?' Trying to sound disinterested.

'Near Ford.'

Did you know your father fired Daniel?'

'No. Dad just said he left.' She took a moment to digest the news. 'Why? Why would he get rid of Daniel?' Had Dad noticed the growing friendship between his daughter and the painter? Was he trying to split them up? He'd wanted Imogen to marry Greg. The two of them were like peas in a pod, when it came to running businesses – or entrepreneurship, as Greg called it.

'Daniel added the stolen plants to the painting because he liked them. Nothing more sinister than that, but I guess the councillor saw the danger. I'm afraid you have to face the fact that your father was breaking the law.'

But not Daniel. At least that was something. 'Will you go to the police?' She crossed her fingers. If he did, Dad's name would be dragged through the mud. She couldn't bear it. She'd only just heard about her father's kinder, more generous side.

'Not about the plants. Daniel lent me some sketches to check, but the plant business doesn't seem to lead anywhere. Unless it supplied a motive I haven't recognised.'

'A falling-out between thieves?'

'Probably not. It seems the rare plant scheme fizzled out years ago.'

'There are no million pound orchids here. I've looked. It's a pity; the hotel could do with a financial boost.'

Adam's face clouded. 'I'd like to go through the hotel accounts with you. Tomorrow, maybe?'

'Of course. Oh, your friend, Maria, will be coming over later to make arrangements for the concert. You know, the concert that magically moved from your garden to mine? Can you come to the meeting?'

'Um.' He hesitated, making a show of looking at his watch.

Imogen was intrigued. Any mention of the Romanian woman threw Adam off balance.

'I'll have to leave it to you, I'm afraid. Josh needs to talk menus.'

Imogen relaxed as he left, some of the weight of anxiety lifted from her shoulders. 'Even though the plant scam could be just the beginning,' she muttered. 'How many other things was Dad up to? And whatever would Mum have thought?'

Imogen's mother had died just after Imogen began at secondary school, soon after her father bought the hotel on profits from the building trade. He became a politician at around the same time.

An annual holiday at Butlin's in Minehead, the highlight of their year, had turned to disaster when her mother had caught a cold that became bronchitis, then pneumonia, and finally took her from the family. Imogen had hated holidays ever since.

If her mother had survived, would Imogen's relationship with her father have improved? She'd never know. Less than a year after his wife died, he stood for election. Once he became a town councillor, he changed.

The first in a string of girlfriends arrived. Imogen had to call her 'Aunt Anna'. Aunt Anna stayed less than a year, replaced by another, younger model. The age of the girlfriends fell, and Imogen became a cross, disobedient teenager, smoking and drinking and hitching her skirts too high, staying out late and answering back when her father objected.

Those 'could do better' reports from school hadn't helped.

A new romance with Susan, a girl only a year or so older than Imogen, proved the final straw. Imogen left home with a sigh of relief, to start her new life at university.

With the twenty-twenty vision of hindsight, Imogen knew her father had been lonely, but his taste for younger women made her skin crawl.

No wonder she'd disliked Emily, the young hotel manager, on sight. Had she been more than an employee to the councillor? With all her heart, Imogen hoped not.

She put her head round the door of the office as she passed, determined to be polite. 'Emily, could you meet with me and Mrs Rostropova at three? I've agreed to help with the charity concert, and it's only a few days away.'

She half hoped Emily would panic or complain, but she just raised an eyebrow and made a note in her online calendar. 'No problem, Mrs Bishop.'

Imogen, oddly disappointed, turned away.

Emily coughed. 'Mrs Bishop, there's something...' She licked her lips.

Imogen had never seen her so uncertain. 'Go on,' she encouraged.

'It's about your father.' The young woman's cheeks were pink. 'The day he had his accident...' A chill travelled up Imogen's spine. 'He had a phone call,' Emily said. 'It came here, through the switchboard. I answered, because Victoria was away from the desk for a moment. A comfort break.'

More likely fixing her make-up. 'What sort of a call?'

'Well, it was a woman. She just asked for... for your father, and I put the call through.

'Did you recognise the voice?' Maria Rostropova, for instance?

Emily shook her head. 'It wasn't anyone I knew.'

'Did my father mention it to you, later?'

'He came down and told me he was going out. He seemed excited. I thought,' she gulped, 'I thought it might be someone he, er, liked.'

'A girlfriend, you mean?'

Emily's blush faded and she smiled the first genuinely warm smile Imogen had seen. 'I didn't want to tell you...'

Imogen would pass the news to Adam tomorrow and maybe, just maybe, rethink her opinion of Emily.

27

ACCOUNTS

'Here.' Next morning, Imogen dumped a pile of paperwork on a desk in front of Adam. 'These are the accounts for the hotel, for the last five years. Emily's on her day off, so she can't help us with questions, but at least no one will be popping in and out of the office. Apart from Harley, of course.' She leaned down and tweaked the dog's ear.

Adam whistled. 'He's a changed dog since he moved over here. I don't know how you manage it. I thought he'd have chewed half the furniture in the hotel by now.'

She threw her head back and laughed. 'He only chews when he's bored. He wrecked your place because you went out and left him, and he was lonely. Didn't you realise that?'

'I've never had a dog. Cats I can handle.'

'That's because they look after themselves. You only have to feed them and let them out from time to time.'

The look of shocked horror on Adam's face sent Imogen into a peal of laughter.

'Cats are the wisest of all animals,' Adam said. 'Far cleverer than humans. They say people own dogs, but cats own people. The Egyptians revered them for their beauty and wisdom.'

Imogen bent down to Harley and, in a stage whisper, murmured, 'Don't you listen. We'll have to teach him about dogs.'

The ex-policeman had a faraway look on his face.

'Adam, why don't you have a cat?'

'I had one, but it was killed. Well, butch— I mean, very violently. I was on the trail of a Cypriot gang, getting too close. They decided to teach me a lesson.'

'I'm sorry. That must have been dreadful.' Was that one of the reasons Adam had left his successful career and buried himself here, in the countryside? Imogen recognised the parallel with her own life – both were searching for healing, in the beauty of this rural setting.

Saying no more, she picked up the first sheet of paper on her pile and frowned, determined to understand the mysteries of company accounts.

Adam followed suit. 'I presume these are the most recent versions?'

Imogen nodded. 'I asked Emily to print them off for us. I hate reading on a computer screen. It makes my eyes itch.'

'I know what you mean. We can delve back further if we need to, but in the meantime, we have plenty to get our teeth into, I see. Now, I'm no expert, but I know what to look out for. I can recognise most of the common red flags for fraud.'

Imogen's teeth were clamped together. 'I'm prepared, don't worry. I know my father was no angel. I'm sure we're going to find plenty of anomalies, and I'm ready for them.'

'Don't panic until you have to. Isn't it the Bible that says, "sufficient to the day is the evil thereof"? Helen Pickles would know. Anyway, let's see what we find and worry about it when we find it.

And, by the way, let's keep the coffee flowing. This could take a very long time.'

'I've told the rest of the staff to bring trays. In fact, here's the first,' as a discreet knock sounded at the door. Imogen fielded a tray piled high with croissants and pastries. 'Thank you,' she smiled at the serious faced young man.

Adam had glanced up. 'Being the boss has its advantages,' he remarked.

'To be honest, I don't really feel in charge here. It's all very new to me.'

'That's because you've let Emily intimidate you. Which is very unlike you, from what I've seen.'

'She knows everything about running a hotel, and I know nothing.'

They sat in silence then, running their fingers down rows of figures.

Adam said, 'I'm looking at what seem to be loans to individuals outside Streamside Ltd. That's something to follow up, but first, I'm getting stuck into that pain au raisin.'

Imogen brushed crumbs aside as she peered over his shoulder. 'There's a loan to your friend, Maria,' she pointed out. She caught sight of his face. 'Why, Adam, I do believe you're blushing.'

'I suppose I'd better come clean,' he said. 'I knew about it. She told me your father loaned her money to help pay a huge debt she'd run up for roof repairs. It didn't cover the full cost, and he'd promised more. Unfortunately, he died before he could fulfil the promise, and she's being hassled by one of the other councillors. He owns the roofing company and he's threatening to sue her. She's scared she'll have to sell the house and have nowhere to live.'

'That's terrible.' Imogen could hardly believe the dramatic, extravagant Maria Rostropova had a care in the world, now she'd manoeuvred Imogen and the hotel into taking on the concert and its arrangements. 'Why didn't you tell me before?'

Adam stroked the top of his head, looking uncomfortable. A spot of red coloured his cheeks. He gave an awkward shrug. 'I assumed the two of them were in a relationship. When we thought your father's death was an accident, it seemed unnecessary to tell you. I thought you'd be upset.'

'Adam,' Imogen laughed, 'one of the reasons I left home and never went back was because of my father's interest in women. He was insatiable. He sometimes had two girlfriends at the same time. You can't tell me anything that would shock me.' She channelled her attention back to the budget statements. A thought struck. 'Is Maria still likely to be sued and have to sell up?'

She had a vision of the Romanian ensconced in The Plough. No, he wouldn't be able to stand it for long. Imogen recognised in Adam a love for independence and time to think. Gardeners and painters, like many who find fulfilment in creative pursuits, needed solitude.

'Adam, admit it. You have a thing for Maria. And,' she developed the thought, 'you've lent her money as well, haven't you?'

'It was either that or watch her try to skim money from the charity concert. Mrs Rostropova has an unusual moral compass, I'm afraid.'

'Well, if you're not rescuing stray dogs, you're taking on life's losers,' Imogen remarked. 'I just hope you don't get your hands burned. Do you seriously think she's going to pay you back?'

'Talking of stray dogs,' Adam changed the subject, but Imogen let it go. 'How's Harley enjoying life at a country house hotel? Is it grand enough for him?'

'He's fabulous,' Imogen grinned. 'He sleeps behind the reception desk most of the time and spends the rest of the day chasing around in the garden, or playing with the staff. I've had to set up a system of fines for anyone who leaves a room without clearing away Harley's soft toys. I'm terrified one of the visitors will trip over one and sue me.'

They worked on, Imogen's eyes blurring as she struggled to follow columns of figures. Sandwiches arrived for lunch, and they munched as they worked. Harley, tiring of their lack of enthusiasm for play, whined at the door until Imogen let him out to help the receptionist greet new arrivals.

Just as Imogen decided she would go blind if she didn't stop and get outside for half an hour, Adam exclaimed, loudly but incoherently.

Imogen said, 'What have you found? More loans?'

'Hm. Not sure, yet. Give me a minute.'

Imogen held her breath. She'd pretended not to mind finding her father was some sort of criminal, but she had to force herself to stay in the room.

The air had turned tense.

Adam placed a few sheets of paper in front of her. 'I've been looking at records for the sale of the hotel to your father. There are a couple of items that we need to check. See, here,' he pointed, 'and here.'

She looked. 'More loans?'

'That's right. But then I found this.' He flipped back through the pile of paperwork. 'Here are the same amounts going in, regularly, apparently from your father's personal account.'

Imogen's stomach rolled. 'Does that mean he's laundering money?'

Adam tapped the fingers of one hand on the desk. 'It could do, but I don't think so. You see, the money's going the wrong way. If he were cleaning up ill-gotten gains, it would be coming into the business account from an outside source and passing on into other outlets. He wouldn't let it anywhere near his personal account. That's asking for trouble.'

'So, what do you think is going on?'

'There's one explanation. You see the payments going out? They're always the same as the money going in, and they go out at regular intervals to one single account.'

Imogen held up one hand. 'Wait, don't tell me. Let me think. Why would Dad pay someone through the business account, with his own money? It's crazy. He's not getting anything in return.'

'Unless...'

The explanation hit Imogen like a train hitting station buffers. 'Blackmail. He's paying someone to keep quiet, and it's going through the hotel accounts because...' she fell silent, still thinking hard. It made no sense. 'Why would he pay through the business? Surely it makes the accounts more complicated?'

'I have an idea.' Adam's face wrinkled. 'He could use his own money to keep the hotel going, if it was going through a bad patch—'

'Which it was,' Imogen put in.

'Quite. Your father was getting on. He was in his eighties, for heaven's sake, and, by all accounts, he didn't live the kind of quiet, retiring life that would keep him fit. He knew he wouldn't be around for ever. Now, if he were paying a blackmailer, presumably he wouldn't want you to know about it, but he knew if he made regular payments to someone, you'd find out about it after he died.'

'So, you think he went through this elaborate reverse laundering just to stop me finding out about his murky past? Why would he even care about that? It's not as though we were close. We hardly even exchanged Christmas cards.' Imogen heard the edge of bitterness in her own voice.

Adam picked up the pile of documents, tapping them sharply on the table to square the edges before he replied, speaking slowly. 'He's still your father. If I'm right, and nothing's certain so far, your father wanted to protect you, either from knowing about his nefarious activities, or because he was afraid for you.'

'Afraid? What do you mean? How can I be in danger from some unknown blackmailer?'

'What if the blackmailer is someone you know?'

Shocked to the core, Imogen took time to process the idea. 'Someone has been blackmailing my father, and it's someone I know?' The turmoil in her stomach built up, until she was scared she would be sick.

'Sit down,' Adam insisted.

Imogen realised she was on her feet, as though about to make a run for the door. She didn't remember standing.

'Don't have more coffee.' Adam removed the pot from her hand, just in time to stop her pouring another cup. 'The caffeine will make you ill.'

Imogen's heart thumped so hard she was surprised Adam couldn't hear it. This must be what a panic attack felt like. Furious with herself, her pride offended – other people had panic attacks, not her.

The office felt claustrophobic. Imogen pushed open the door and Harley, ears pricked, clattered across the foyer, made a beeline for Imogen and leaned against her. Trying to slow her thumping heartbeat, she tickled him behind a front leg. He leaned harder.

She muttered, 'I need to think this through. There must be a mistake.'

Adam waited.

'I'm going to have to reconcile this view of my father,' she announced. 'All the time we were ignoring each other, he was worried about me. If I think about it, I'm not really surprised he was being blackmailed. He wasn't bothered by a bit of illegality. For one thing, there's the rare plants scam...' She stopped talking as another thought struck.

Adam raised an eyebrow. 'Have you thought of something?'

Breathing steadily, the panic retreating a little, Imogen managed a smile. 'It's nothing. I just need to think all this through. It's been something of a bombshell.'

'Can I help?'

'No.' The last thing she needed was sympathy. She softened her tone. 'I mean, thanks, but I'll just take Harley for a run in the garden. I always think better out of doors.'

28

EARRING

As Adam left, Imogen turned back into the office, grateful for his understanding. She swivelled the computer screen round and clicked the mouse several times. Immediately, a list appeared of the day's guests. She clicked on the little calendar icon at the top of the screen, worked her way back to the week of her father's death, and printed out the names and addresses of everyone staying at the hotel.

Harley panting with excitement at her heels, the list in her pocket, Imogen strolled through the hotel and out into the garden, maintaining as calm an exterior as possible. The air in the garden was blessedly warm, scented with the perfume from early roses, but its charms were wasted on Imogen.

She drew in a deep breath. Her mind raced, full of thoughts she couldn't ignore. What if her father was killed because of the rare plant business? Oswald, the gardener, had realised something illegal was going on, but most visitors to the hotel or local guests would have no idea there was anything odd about the plants. They were just ordinary flowers, growing anonymously in an obscure corner of the carefully managed grounds of the Streamside Hotel.

Imogen sank onto on an old wooden bench by the stream. She'd sat here often, watching Daniel paint.

She shook the thought away. No time for that.

She spread the lists on the bench, weighting them down with stones. She'd have to find somewhere more comfortable to sit, if she intended to spend so much thinking time out here. Maybe a cushion?

She ran a finger down the list on the first page, murmuring names aloud, testing them for familiarity, but none rang a bell. It seemed everyone on the list was a complete stranger. Imogen had not even been at the hotel the week her father died, so she couldn't even match a face to any name.

She turned to the second sheet and repeated the process, more mechanically, with less eager expectation.

She stopped and hesitated. Here, at last, was a name that rang a bell. Imogen muttered it aloud once more and remembered. It was a mildly famous actor, one who'd been in a TV drama. Not *Broadlands*, she thought, or *Happy Valley*. She closed her eyes and recalled the actor had taken small parts in either *Midsomer Murders* or *Lewis*. That was it. The handsome, dark eyed suspect in a *Lewis* episode. Fancy his staying at the hotel.

She continued down the list, wishing she'd been around then. The actor was quite the heartthrob, with a magnificent physique and one of those little boy smiles Imogen recognised. Some men used that look to disarm their wives when they were lying. Greg had tried it, often, never realising Imogen was no longer fooled.

Imogen reached the final page. Her gaze slid down the last few lines. She was already half on her feet, ready to give up, when a name seemed to jump from the page. David Canberra. He'd been one of the boys she knew from the boys' school.

Excitement rising in the pit of her stomach, Imogen scrambled to her feet. She couldn't remember much about David, apart from his friendship with Julian, but he'd been there, that night, in the tunnel, and she had his address. She blessed the legal requirement for hotels to keep records. She didn't care if she was breaking data protection laws by using the information for her own purposes. This was a connection to her father's death.

Why would David be staying at the hotel? Surely, he had friends or family in the town. Perhaps he didn't want anyone to know he was here. Or, had her father invited him? Was he involved in the plant scam?

No, she was getting ahead of the evidence. Just as well Adam wasn't around to point that out.

Still, if David, who she recalled as a tall but weedy teenager, with a gap between his front teeth, had something to do with her father's death, that meant Daniel wasn't the culprit. Voicing the idea that he could be, even in her own head, terrified Imogen. Anyone but Daniel. That had been the reason for her embarrassing panic attack – the fear that Daniel was involved.

Much better it should be David Canberra.

She took a breath.

David Canberra lived in Cornwall. There was no time to drive that far today, but tomorrow...

Harley barked, breaking into her thoughts.

She looked up, but he was out of sight.

'Harley,' she called, but no dog scurried towards her. Thrusting the lists into her bag, she set off in pursuit as the dog barked again. 'I'm coming. What's the matter, you silly animal?'

Harley's tail waved in the air as he scrabbled at the earth beside the orangery.

In moments, Imogen was by his side, sickened. Her husband's body had lain only a few feet away. She hadn't been back to the building since the police left. She was thinking of tearing the structure down, replacing it with a tree, something in memory of Greg. She owed him that, at least.

She shrieked at Harley. 'What are you doing? Get away.'

The dog looked up and waited, one paw in the air.

Imogen swallowed hard, wishing she could run back into the hotel. 'What have you found?'

Harley barked again, rigid as stone, nose pointing at the earth.

Something glinted in the sunlight. Imogen crouched low. She scrabbled the object from the earth. An earring.

'Not one of mine. What on earth is it doing here?'

She held the small pearl in the palm of her hand, its gold clasp bright in the sun. How did it find its way to this spot?

She sat back on her heels, thinking hard. She was sure she'd seen it before.

She gasped as she remembered. Steph had worn a pair of earrings like this to the reunion.

When had she been in the garden?

'How very odd.'

Harley still stood at doggy attention.

Imogen delved into her pocket and pulled out a dog treat. 'Here you are. Well done.'

She tossed the treat to Harley, ignored his pleas for another, and let him follow her up to her bedroom.

How had Steph's earring found its way to the orangery?

Another mystery. There were so many, but perhaps she was getting close. Means, motive, opportunity; did they fit? What did this earring tell her?

She'd spoken out loud. Harley looked at her expectantly. She pocketed the earring, left the hotel, and crossed the lane to The Plough, Harley at her heels.

She peeped through the window to Adam's sitting room. He

stood by his easel; face wrinkled in concentration. Was it fair to bother him? She'd shrugged off his offer of help and sent him home. It would serve her right if he told her to get lost.

She'd leave and tell him about her strange discovery later.

It was too late. Harley had other ideas. He shoved the door open and leaped inside, tugging Imogen across the floor.

Adam grabbed the easel to stop it falling, while Imogen pulled on Harley's lead.

'Sorry. He took me by surprise. He's pleased to see you.'

Adam bent over and scratched behind Harley's ear, but his gaze rested on Imogen's face. 'Hello, again. I've missed you, too. It must be an hour since I left the hotel.'

'I'm sorry. You're busy and I've disturbed you. I'll take Harley away and let you paint.'

Adam smiled, loaded a brush with red paint, and swept it across his canvas. 'I was joking. I'll paint, you talk. Just stop this animal eating my work, will you? You seem to have news. What's happened?'

'A funny thing. I don't know whether it's important, but it's odd.' She fell silent, watching Adam's brush moving rhythmically across the empty canvas. The effect was calming. What on earth was he painting with all that red?

'Go on. I'm intrigued.'

She'd tell him about the earring in a moment. She had to ask, 'What exactly is that painting meant to be?'

'It's going to be the village. Lower Hembrow. I'm planning to fit your hotel and my pub in the same composition.' He waved a hand at the canvas. 'This red is called under-painting. I believe it's meant to give the picture a warm glow, according to one of the highly priced books I bought. I'm planning to paint the buildings over the wash, and it will look as though the evening sun's shining.' He grinned. 'I'm not so sure. I'd like to stand outside to paint, but I don't want anyone watching my pathetic splatterings.'

'Oh, I'm sorry. I'll go—'

'I don't mean you. You're welcome. Now,' he used the rag on his hands, 'you have me on tenterhooks. What strange thing happened to you in the garden?'

Imogen told him the details of Harley's discovery. 'I can think of a way the earring found its way there,' she added, 'but I don't like it.'

'Mm.' Adam scratched his cheek, leaving a streak of red paint. 'Tell me your theory.'

'Not yet. I need to think it through, first.'

* * *

Adam washed his hands. There was no time for more painting. He looked around the room. Intended to be his bolt hole, where he painted and enjoyed his so-called retirement, it was filling quickly with evidence from this new, fast growing investigation.

A row of files stood on the console table at the side of the room that had recently held his coffee maker. They were filled, partly with documents relating to the hotel, but also with the plant sketches he'd taken from Daniel. He'd pass it all on to DCI Andrews, but not yet. He'd reported his theories about the councillor's death to the authorities, and Andrews had taken them less than seriously.

Adam wrinkled his nose in disgust. Proper policing, the DCI had said, but hadn't bothered with the hotel's records.

Adam made a promise to himself. He would see this case through to the end.

And what if, a little voice in his head wondered, *what if Imogen's secret love, Daniel, turns out to be the villain?* Adam felt oddly protective of Imogen. He'd grown fond of her so quickly. She'd become his best friend – he felt closer to her than to that unobtainable goddess, Maria.

Daniel wasn't the only suspect. There was another, even less welcome.

'No, not that,' he groaned aloud.

A murderer, no matter who, must be apprehended and put away, safely, at Her Majesty's pleasure. Justice – that was central to his moral code.

Collateral damage was irrelevant.

He shrugged into his coat. He needed to dig his way to the bottom of this case, as soon as possible, or even worse things could happen.

Imogen's head whirled with information. She pushed the earring puzzle out of her head. Instead, she would focus on the unexpected revelations about her father. He had cared about her, after all. He'd been up to all sorts of illegality, but Imogen could forgive him, now.

Suddenly cheerful, she relished the next few hours she planned to spend at Haselbury House, well away from any mysterious deaths.

Her heavy boots were already in the car. She ran downstairs, Harley galloping enthusiastically at her feet. 'Just make sure you behave. Don't eat the plants, and don't go digging up any more finds.'

As she hurtled through the foyer, Emily stopped her in her tracks. 'Mrs Bishop.'

Imogen halted, Harley skidding past on the polished floor.

'Mrs Bishop, there's someone to see you. In the lounge.'

Imogen cursed under her breath. 'Who is it?' She crossed her fingers. Not the police. She'd have to talk to them again soon, but not today, please.

'Someone called Steph Aldred.'

Steph? What was she doing here? Anger sparked, and a stab of fear. Steph and Daniel had been together at the reunion; were they an item? Had Steph come here to warn Imogen off Daniel.

She cast a longing look at the door but turned into the lounge.

'Hello. What can I do for you?'

Steph, who'd always been small for her age, didn't seem to have grown much since leaving school. She struggled from the depths of a hotel sofa.

'Imogen.' Steph held out a hand, and Imogen took it. The fingers felt long and cool. Steph said, 'I didn't really get to talk to you at the reunion. I wanted to say how sorry I was about Greg. I mean, I know things weren't great between the two of you, but still, it must have been a dreadful shock.'

Imogen struggled with her feelings. Steph had always been the kindest, most gentle of her friends, but now?

'Thank you,' she managed. 'It's all been... very difficult.'

'And your father died, as well. So sad.' Steph's eyes looked into Imogen's; her expression guileless.

She was about to blurt out the news that her father had been murdered, too. She caught herself in time. No one knew that, apart from Adam. Imogen spoke with care. 'It's good of you to come,' she said. 'It sounds horribly rude, I know, but I have to leave. I'm still working at—'

'Haselbury House. I know. I saw the photo spread in *This Somerset*.'

Imogen remembered. Steph had studied English at university and gone on to work on a local newspaper. In fact, hadn't she moved on to one of the national papers? 'Are you back in Somerset permanently?'

Steph nodded. 'I came back to write my own books. I was tired of journalism; working on one story after another for the paper. They gave me the female jobs, like interviewing women of achievement, and I realised I hadn't achieved any of my own goals. I always wanted to write fiction, but I kept putting it on the back burner. Then, I was sent to interview Daniel about his work, and he convinced me to... well, it sounds corny, but to follow my own dreams. Like he had. So, that's what I did. I came back—'

'To your parents' old house?'

'They died a few years ago, and it's mine, now.'

'That's great. I'm very pleased for you, but I really have to go. Let's get together for a drink. Are you free tomorrow night?' What was she doing? Why had she said that? It was like picking a scab, wanting to see the two of them together. She'd only torture herself with jealousy.

It was too late. Steph beamed. 'I'd love to. Shall we go over the road, or do you avoid the rival establishment?'

'Not at all. Adam Hennessy and I are friends.'

No harm in taking Steph to The Plough. Adam might pick up useful information from her.

* * *

As Imogen approached the stately home in all its shabby grandeur, she wondered why Steph had called. Was she scratching around for information about Greg? Or perhaps, Imogen thought as she heaved gardening kit from the boot of her car, she was innocently looking for characters for her novel. In which case, Imogen hoped she would look elsewhere.

Still, the evening should prove interesting. She'd take the earring along.

'Mrs Bishop, you're a welcome sight.' The new owner of Haselbury House, a stout, burly man with a red drinkers' nose, brought his top-of-the-range Range Rover to a halt at her side. 'Bit of a prob with the fountain, I'm afraid.'

'Fountain? There isn't one.'

'Sure, there is – twenty feet tall, cascading down a wall—'

'It's a waterfall.'

This man had far too much money and precious little common sense.

He introduced the lead contractor organising the heavy digging.

'It's that there woodland,' the contractor pointed. 'We chopped down a few of them lovely old trees.' He shot a black look at the owner. 'Beauties, they were. Oak and ash. Mind you, the ash had a touch of dieback, so it would have had to go—'

'Yes, yes. Let's get to the point,' the owner interrupted.

'Ah, fair enough. Once the trees had gone, and we'd pulled down the old cottage that had been there for centuries...' The owner was brushing mud from his car. The contractor glowered at his back. 'We found a lot of little crosses and suchlike in the ground. Seems the family used to bury their pets in the clearing. Can't put the waterfall there, can we? Would have all the locals up in arms.'

He grunted. 'Pity no one bothered to tell us about them earlier. No cooperation. You'd think local people didn't want a visitor attraction in the area to pull in the crowds.'

Perhaps the neighbours enjoyed a quiet life.

Imogen let it pass.

Harley had found an interesting scent. Imogen called him away and held up a warning finger. 'If you dig anything up here, you'll be sent straight off to the kennels. Understand?'

She spent an hour with the contractor, Jim, staring at maps, drawing lines, and shading areas, until they'd designed a new configuration for the water feature that avoided the pet cemetery.

'That owner, he's a townie, through and through,' the contractor complained. 'Still, he's not tight with the cash, I'll grant him that. Made his fortune in one of those computer start-ups and sold the business before the latest stock market crash. Lucky beggar. Money coming out of his ears. Anything we suggest is OK with him.' He winked and stomped off on foot to explain the new plans to his team.

* * *

The owner treated Imogen to a sumptuous lunch. Harley was banned from the dining room. He stood at the door, doing his best to look ill-treated, until certain Imogen had no intention of letting him in.

'Sorry about that business with the site,' the owner said. 'We've dug up so much of the ground, I lost track. Had no idea what was buried there, but when we knocked down the old cottage in the woods, we found a couple of bits of wood with names on: Spot, Blaze, and some others. Pets, you see. I rang a mate of mine, Jonathan, who knew the original owners, and he confirmed it. The whole area was an animal cemetery—' He stopped, abruptly. 'I'm sorry, that must be painful for you to hear – with your husband dying in the grounds of your hotel.'

Was that his idea of tact?

Imogen took a breath and changed the subject. 'We can work around it.' She showed him the revised design.

Something the new owner had said clicked in her brain. 'Did you say Jonathan?' she queried. 'Do you mean Jonathan Hampton? Whose family owned Streamside Manor before my father bought it?'

'That's the man. Jonathan's father was big buddies with the Jenkins that owned this place.'

'That's a bit of a coincidence.'

'Not really. These rural hunting and shooting families all know each other; half of them have inter-married. The Jenkins and the Hamptons used to be thick as thieves.'

Imogen flinched at the phrase.

'In fact, your father, the councillor—' He stopped talking, His mouth hung open. What had he been about to say?

'Go on.' Imogen gave a rueful chuckle. 'My father...?'

'Well,' the owner tugged at his beard, avoiding her eye. 'I heard some local gossip, going back thirty years or so, about the deal he made when he bought the hotel. Folk say other buyers were frozen out, had their planning permission refused, that sort of thing. All a long time ago. Nothing in it, I'm sure. Perfectly normal transactions.' He pulled out his iPhone. 'If you'll excuse me, I have to get on. I'll leave you to give instructions about the new position for the fountain.'

'Waterfall,' Imogen corrected automatically.

The owner was gone in a moment. Imogen followed him out and sought out Harley. He was helping the contractors dig foundations.

'I reckon the owner of this place has been mixed up in whatever financial hanky panky my father cooked up with all these Jenkins and Hamptons.' She told him. 'I'm starting to wonder if everyone in this part of Somerset is on the take.'

'Harley, the garden's beginning to wake up.'

Harley bounded into the garden the next day, ever hopeful of catching rabbits. The sun had barely risen above the row of hawthorns lining the stream as Imogen, in jeans, jumper and a gilet, hair bundled into a rough ponytail under a straw hat, pulled on her wellies and chased the dog into the soft morning air.

'Wait for me.'

Harley bounded towards the orangery. Imogen's throat tightened. When would she be ready to go back in there? Would she ever forget Greg's body, slumped on the floor?

If she couldn't enjoy the orangery, she'd get on with planting out summer flowering perennials. They wouldn't flower much in the next few months, but they'd put down roots and flourish next year.

The potting shed smelled of earth. Imogen breathed deeply. Oswald was already there.

'Do you ever sleep?' she asked.

Harley, recognising the gardener as a soft touch, sat at his feet and raised a paw.

'He's getting fat,' Imogen pointed out, as Oswald fed treats to Harley.

'I reckon he can carry a few extra pounds. Such a skinny creature he was, before he came to the hotel. You've worked wonders, miss. That Adam Hennessy, he knows nothing about dogs.'

'He's a cat person.'

'Is he now?' Oswald stroked his chin with earth stained fingers. 'That gives me an idea.'

'Spill the beans.'

'The man needs a companion.'

'Given the choice, I think he'd go for Maria Rostropova.'

Oswald chuckled so hard, Imogen feared he would choke. 'That woman – she knows how to get her way. Young Adam should steer clear of her.'

'Young?'

'Aye, the man's young compared with me and the missus.'

'Tell me more about Maria. She's persuaded me to hold her concert here.'

'Yes, the woman's got her claws into you, too. Mind you, local folk think the concert's a grand idea. I popped in for milk at the shop and I heard Mrs Croft tell Edwina Topsham she thought you'd fitted nicely into the village.'

'She did?' Imogen tried not to beam. People didn't hate her, then. Why had she assumed they would?

'Better than that husband of yours – rest his soul,' Oswald added as an afterthought.

'Greg?'

'Came here too often, if you ask me,' Oswald grumbled.

Imogen raised herself to her full height. 'He was only buried a few days ago. We should be—'

'Respectful?' The old man cackled, ending with fit of productive, pipe smoker's coughing. 'When you get to my age, you've no time for pretending. Your husband was a bad lot, my girl, and that's the truth.'

'What do you mean?' Did she really want to know? Imogen braced herself.

'Why'd he come here every few weeks without you? Business with your dad?' Oswald huffed. 'I reckon it were that hotel manager he came to see.'

'Emily?'

'That's right. What those two got up to – well, I wouldn't like to say.'

Emily and Greg? Why hadn't Imogen realised? Greg had told her they were business trips. She'd long known he was unfaithful, but with Emily?

She didn't want to hear any more. 'We'd better get on,' she muttered.

'Aye, he's gone, now, your Greg. Best you look elsewhere.'

Something tickled Imogen's ear. She brushed it away with one hand and screamed.

'Oswald – it's a spider – get it away from me.'

'Just a little one. Won't hurt you.' He picked it off her shoulder and held out his clenched hand.

'Get rid of it, please,' she pleaded.

The old man cackled and coughed. 'You and your old dad – both of you gardeners, and both scared of a little spider.' He threw it outside, crossed the shed to a row of shelves and pulled down a bag of fertiliser.

A line of bags occupied the highest shelf, each one bearing the bright yellow symbol for poison. 'What are those?' Imogen pointed.

'Just a spot of rat poison and a few traps. Nasty creatures, rats. Get everywhere. Come in the shed, they do, after my seeds.' He grunted. 'I just leave a few granules of the stuff in a trap. That finishes off the little beasts.'

Imogen squinted at the ingredients on the back of a packet. She wasn't about to touch it. One word caught her attention. 'Brodifacoum? Oswald, this is the poison that killed my husband. Did the police see it?'

He shrugged. 'They took a bag away and gave me the third degree. Did I follow the health and safety guidelines? Do I ever – I keep the shed locked. I showed them where I keep the key, in the cupboard up in the hotel. It's more than my job's worth to break the rules – your father would have fired me on the spot.'

He went back to sifting compost into an array of pots. As she watched; a cloud of depression settled on Imogen. The police had found poison on her property – yet another reason to suspect her of murder.

Adam pulled pints in The Plough as Imogen arrived. 'The choir are in. They'll be singing soon,' he said. 'It's likely to get rowdy. Those baritones can drink me under the table any time. Not to mention Benjamin Bunny.'

'Sorry? Who?'

'Their conductor – or musical director, as he likes to be known. His name's Benjamin Boniface, but he hops around like a rabbit. All enthusiasm. Look at him, now.'

The conductor, a man of around forty, with a substantial girth, a pink face and a pair of glasses that constantly slipped down his nose, bounded from one singer to another. He pulled on their sleeves, hurrying them towards the piano. 'Let's get started. No time to waste,' he urged.

Imogen surveyed the drinkers in the corner. 'I can't imagine you're much of a drinker, Adam. More of an observer.'

'Dead right. Never could manage more than a pint or two. I see you've left Harley behind. Has he been misbehaving?'

'Actually, no. I took him to work with me yesterday and I had an interesting talk with the owner at Haselbury. I'll tell you about it sometime. I can see you're busy, now. Oh, and here's Steph.'

'Steph?' Adam followed Imogen's gaze.

Steph Aldred made her way to the bar. 'Hello, good to see you again.' She looked more attractive than ever, and at least ten years younger than her age.

Imogen raised an eyebrow. 'You two know each other?'

Steph said, 'We only met once. Mr Hennessy called round about something.'

'Did he?' Imogen frowned. He hadn't mentioned it.

She shared a glance with Adam and he gave a little shake of the head.

She wouldn't mention the earring yet. If Steph had left it in the garden, she'd have a story ready – and Imogen wanted to think more about why Steph, or anyone else, would leave it beside the orangery.

She was learning to trust nobody.

* * *

Helen, the vicar, seated at the piano, played a few stirring chords and the choir launched into a cheerful rendition of 'It's Raining Men'.

The Plough patrons joined in with gusto.

As they finished, Adam served more beer and set a plate of salty cheese snacks on the piano.

'Thirsty work,' the conductor enthused, holding his pint glass aloft.

'And builds up an appetite,' the vicar agreed.

Once everyone was served, the choir sang a quieter number. The crowd at the bar thinned, leaving Imogen and Steph within

Adam's earshot. He kept his ears open. If he happened to over-hear their conversation, that was simply coincidence. Wasn't it?

'It's about that night at school.' Steph's head was close to Imogen. She spoke softly.

Adam kept his eyes on the glasses he was polishing, and the counter that needed wiping down, and concentrated. He could just make out what the two women said.

He recognised Imogen's cool tone, the one she used when holding people at arm's length.

'It was a stupid prank,' she was saying, 'and it ended badly for poor Julian.'

'Exactly. It was terrible. We all went our separate ways, and nobody talked about what happened.'

'It was just an accident...'

Steph's eyes flashed. 'Come on, Imogen. You're not that naive. Maybe then, we wanted to believe it was an accident, but I've been a journalist for years. I can sniff out secrets, and I know when someone's pulling the wool over my eyes.' She looked directly at Adam and pointed to her glass. 'Perhaps you'd kindly pour us each another glass of wine, Mr Hennessy, since you happen to be close by. Mine's a Pinot Grigio.'

Adam, chastened at having been so easily caught eavesdrop-ping, poured wine. 'It's on the house.'

'Well, you won't make your fortune that way,' Steph said, tartly.

Steph nodded her thanks as he set the glasses on the bar.

Imogen said, 'It's all right, Steph. Adam knows what's going on. He's been helping me get to the bottom of Greg's murder. Although, we haven't got very far.'

'Well, I don't think I can help with that, as I told you, Mr Hennessy, when you visited.' Steph turned to Imogen. 'We should have talked about Julian. How could his death have been an acci-dent? We had lights, and no one was running or pushing. Why would Julian fall and hit his head so hard it killed him? I think the police let it go because we were all so young and Julian's parents didn't make a fuss. They were far too timid. I thought it was time we cleared the air.'

Imogen bit her lip.

'You mean, it was you who set up that evening?'

'Afraid so. I wanted to rattle a few cages and talk about what happened. I got in touch with Mrs Hall and suggested a reunion for the whole of our year. You know how teachers enjoy that kind of thing. She tracked people down. I think she's lonely and living in the past. Kate and I had been in touch a few times over the years, so I knew where she was. If you hadn't thrown a wobbly and left early, we might have got further.'

Imogen gazed at the floor, cheeks aflame.

Steph either did not see or did not care. 'Anyway, I talked to a few of the others, that evening, and found out a few things.'

Imogen's head jerked up. 'You did?'

'I discovered Julian and David were an item.'

'What?' Imogen's mouth fell open, her eyes wide. 'You mean...'

'Kate saw them in the cinema, sitting together and holding hands.'

Imogen was shaking her head. 'But... but Julian asked me out.'

'Trying to prove he wasn't gay. Although, we didn't call it that in those days. You were the prettiest girl in the class, so he asked you out to cover his tracks.'

Just at that moment of peak revelation, Adam was called away. The beer barrel needed changing. Disappointed, he dragged himself down to the cellar. As he went, he heard Steph say, 'And that's why he died. David was jealous and they had a fight. Julian wasn't much of a fighter and David gave him a few hard punches. I reckon that fight killed him.'

'We'd like to talk to you again.' A young, moon faced detective constable with over-gelled hair, pointed shoes and a smug smile tapped his fingers on the desk in the hotel foyer. A mix of guests milled around, open-mouthed.

'They think she murdered her husband.' The eager whisper echoed through the space.

Imogen had known this moment would come, but nothing had prepared her for the fear. Her throat filled with bile. Was she about to be arrested and charged with Greg's murder? Had the police even looked in any other direction?

A camera phone flashed.

Time to move out of the public eye.

'Please come into the office.'

Emily scuttled out, pink with excitement. 'Coffee?' she offered.

Imogen glared. 'Not just now.'

In the office, she sat at a desk and nodded at the constable.

'How can I help you?'

'We'd like you to come to the station again. Now, if possible.'

'Couldn't you have telephoned instead of making me a spectacle in front of all the hotel guests?'

The constable's smile faltered. 'Sorry, just doing what the boss asked.'

'Detective Chief Inspector Andrews?' Imogen's stomach churned.

'Yes, ma'am. I can take you in the car if you like...' Apologetic.

Imogen shrugged. 'How will I get home again? Or are you planning to lock me up?'

'No, no – I mean, that's not my decision, ma'am.'

'Well, I'll follow in my own car once I've spoken to my solicitor.'

'Oh, that won't—'

'It most certainly will be necessary. Tell your boss I'll be there in an hour.'

He made for the door, his neck pink. Imogen regretted snapping at him. He was only a young lad.

'Would you like that coffee before you go? Emily will get one for you.'

He perked up as she waved Emily in.

Imogen sped upstairs. In the privacy of her room, she telephoned the fearsome Sheila Brooks.

The solicitor sounded breathless. 'You've just caught me, I'm in and out of court today, but I can spare an hour.'

Imogen tried to call Adam but reached his answer phone. 'The police want me at the station. Can you come?'

She clicked her tongue. That sounded pathetic.

She rang again. 'Sorry, I panicked. Don't worry about it. I'll tell you what happens when I get back.'

If they let me go.

* * *

Time crawled. The hard, tiled bench in the police station gave Imogen backache. She turned her coat collar up to shut out the ripe-smelling youth on her left. He rocked back and forth, in his own world, one finger exploring his mouth for food scraps.

The young DC ushered Imogen into the interview room where Detective Chief Inspector Andrews and Sheila Brooks were sharing a joke.

The DCI smiled, eyebrows under control. This wasn't going to last long, he just wanted to clear up a few points.

'I thought you'd prefer to come here again, to avoid a fuss at your hotel.'

That was thoughtful – but a pity he hadn't made that point to his constable.

'When did you last see your father?' he asked.

'I'm sorry?'

She gathered her wits. So this wasn't about Greg?

'Boxing Day.' Greg had been there with her, exchanging whisky and business gossip with her father. Imogen had offered a carefully chosen plant encyclopaedia as a gift in the hope of building bridges, but her father had barely glanced at it, dropping it on a side table like a hot potato.

'Did you keep in touch by telephone?'

'Texts, sometimes.'

'And these were about...'

'Nothing much. You know, when one of us went on holiday, or birthdays. That was about it. I'm afraid we weren't close.'

Sheila Brooks frowned. 'Don't volunteer anything,' she'd said.

The questioning turned to her father's car, its service record and how often he changed it.

Imogen blurted out, 'You think he was murdered, then?'

The DCI replied, speaking slowly, clearly choosing his words with care. 'We have reason to suspect the car crash may have been less than accidental.' He coughed. 'I imagine you've discussed this with your neighbour, Mr Hennessy.'

The solicitor sat up, suddenly alert. It seemed she'd heard of Adam.

The DCI continued, 'Please tell us where you were on...' from his notebook, he read out the date of her father's death, 'on 20th March.' She'd been at Haselbury House, that day.

There were other questions, but she could answer very few.

Did the police know about her father's illicit import and export of restricted plants? She longed to tell them everything she'd discovered, to convince them she was holding nothing back, but she couldn't. Daniel had painted the hotel garden and those flowers, and Adam knew it. Had he told the police? How much did they know? Could Daniel possibly be involved in her father's death? She shivered. Surely not.

At last, the DCI drew the interview to a close, reiterated his condolences for her losses, and asked her to sign a witness statement the constable was preparing, based on the interview. And that was all.

Sheila Brooks gave her a nod and an unexpectedly friendly wink.

She was free to go.

Shaky, in need of the strongest coffee the hotel could supply, Imogen couldn't wait to leave the police station. In her haste, she failed to notice Adam in the foyer.

He called after her, 'I got your message. Are you all right?'

* * *

He took a long look at Imogen's face and prescribed a hot drink. 'The coffee in police stations is terrible, but it does the job.' He pointed at a machine. 'You wait here. I've organised a meeting with DCI Andrews. I'll only be a minute.'

'Well,' DCI Andrews said, crossing his legs comfortably. 'I see you've come charging in to your friend's rescue.'

'Not at all.' Adam was too experienced a copper to let Andrews tweak his nose. 'There's new information.'

'And, does Mrs Bishop know this? Because she's giving remarkably little away, if so.'

'Do you blame her? She knows she's at the top of your list of suspects for her husband's murder.'

'She's right, but that wasn't what we discussed today.'

'No?' Adam let the word hang in the air, but Andrews didn't elaborate. Adam leaned back in his chair. 'Well, you might be interested in some gossip I heard. It's no more than that, but it puts a whole new complexion on the councillor's activities.'

'Does it indeed?'

Adam saw enthusiasm spark in the other man's eyes. He thought for a moment. Imogen had told him about her trip to the stately home and the information she'd gleaned from the new owner, after Steph had left The Plough last night. Had she passed it on to the police? He doubted it. He'd be willing to bet she'd said as little as possible.

'I run a pub and I listen to the gossip.' Adam recounted the stately homeowner's suspicions about property price fixing and mentioned the funds passing in and out of the hotel accounts.

DCI Andrews laughed. 'We're on to that. It seems someone was blackmailing the good councillor. Trouble is, blackmailers don't usually kill off their victims, so that doesn't help much with our murder inquiry.'

At least he agreed it was a murder.

'But you've given us a few pointers. Like everyone else involved, you're holding back, but we can find you if we need to talk further. We'd heard something of the councillor's activities, and we may have enough to round up a few of his cronies soon.'

'That's great. What about the other murder?'

A silence fell.

The DCI blinked, frowned, coughed and fiddled with his pen. 'Another murder? Your friend's husband and father aren't enough for you?'

'Well, anything I can do to help, you just need to let me know.'

Andrews' eyebrows twitched. 'What's this other death? Why don't I know about it?'

'It's a cold case from thirty years ago. It was dropped – the whole thing looked like a teenage prank, kids drinking and tripping over each other in a dark tunnel in the middle of the night. The investigation concluded the young lad's death was no more than a tragic accident.'

Adam searched for the right words. He needed to persuade Andrews to take Julian's death seriously and reopen the case, but he was close to retirement and happy with a quiet life behind a desk. Much easier to brush a long-buried cold case under the carpet.

'The people involved that night included your murder victim, Gregory Bishop, his widow, Imogen – who also happens to be the surviving daughter of murder victim number two – and a motley bunch of their friends and acquaintances.'

He let the information sink in.

'Now, to misquote Oscar Wilde, one death may be a misfortune, but a second is carelessness – and a third suggests something entirely more sinister.'

DCI Andrews swallowed hard, his Adam's apple jerking in his throat. 'Are you seriously suggesting there's a serial killer on the loose in Somerset?'

'Not really. Not in the sense of a murderer who kills from a compulsion to do so, or from cruelty, or sadism, or any peculiar sexual motive. No, I believe these three murders were all committed by the same person for another reason. And, until we can understand that reason, we're going to have all sorts of problems pinning down the culprit.'

The DCI let out a long, low groan. 'Where's the evidence? I'm not moving scarce resources back to a closed case from thirty years ago without a watertight reason. Greg Bishop is our only definite murder. Unless you can convince me, without a shadow of a doubt, I'm sticking to the councillor's death as either some kind of villainous tit-for-tat with his nefarious criminal colleagues, or an accident. This pie-in-the-sky ghost from the past you've brought me is an entirely unrelated accident, unless you prove otherwise.'

'Fair enough.' All Adam could do was hope this conversation set off a spark of interest with the DCI. Enough for him to look at the case file. Perhaps his mind would open by just an inch or two. The man was no fool.

'If you find any real evidence, the kind we can show to the Crown Prosecution Service don't hesitate to bring it to me.' Andrews threw a long look at Adam and offered the tiniest nod.

Adam understood. The DCI wanted him to keep on the case, unofficially.

The DCI scraped back his chair and lumbered to his feet. 'Thank you, by the way. You've been most helpful in this business of the councillor's car crash.'

Adam left, satisfied.

He checked his watch. He'd been here longer than intended. Would Imogen still be waiting?

There was no sign of Imogen in the reception area so Adam ran out into the car park. At that moment, Imogen backed her car into the busy main road outside the station. She reversed fast and a car horn hooted.

Adam shook his head, opening his car door. Imogen did nothing by halves.

An engine revved madly, and a black SUV sped up the road, overtaking the line of cars, avoiding oncoming traffic by inches, and settled into place with just a blue Peugeot between it and Imogen.

Adam started his engine and roared into the road.

33

CHASE

Grimly, Adam pulled in behind the Peugeot. The SUV driver might be innocently going about his business, but no sense in taking a chance.

The convoy left the main road and took a quieter route. The SUV dropped back. Now, there were two cars between Imogen and the SUV. Maybe Adam was worrying unnecessarily.

The Peugeot turned off. Directly behind the SUV, now, Adam caught a glimpse of the driver. Yellow jacket. Black hair in a ponytail.

The driver was a woman.

Brakes squealed. Imogen skidded sharp left, no signal, leaving a puff of exhaust.

The SUV braked hard, on Imogen's heels, dropping any pretence of innocence.

The new track wound through hedgerows, the road muddy but passable.

Adam signalled, turned, and stood on the brake, screeching to a halt just inches from the SUV.

Imogen leapt out, running towards the SUV, fury contorting her face. Adam flung open his door, yelling at her to stop.

Too late.

She'd reached the SUV and was hammering on the driver's window. 'How dare you?'

Adam arrived seconds later, as the SUV's door flew open and the driver emerged.

Imogen ignored Adam. An accusing finger pointed at the other woman.

The SUV driver muttered, 'I wasn't... I mean, I didn't...'

'What's going on?' Adam asked, bewildered.

Imogen snapped, 'Toni's been spying on me.' Anger flashed in her eyes. 'Why are you trailing me?'

The driver stammered. 'Honestly, Imogen, there's no need to overreact. I thought we should talk.'

Imogen's high-pitched laugh grated on Adam's ears. Her hands were clenched, her body shaking with fury, as though a dam of self-control had finally burst inside, and she was on the attack. 'Talk? What about? What do you want with me?'

Adam raised a hand, his voice soothing, conciliating. 'Let's all take a step back and calm down.'

With a visible effort, Imogen wrenched her gaze away from Toni.

'You saw, Adam. She was chasing me.'

'I agree, she was – but no harm done. Maybe she has an explanation?'

'It had better be good.'

Time to step in again before they came to blows. 'Let's get back to Lower Hembrow and talk this over.' He spoke directly to Toni. 'You have some explaining to do. I watched you follow Mrs Bishop. I presume you're the Toni who invited her to that class reunion?'

'And who do you think you are?' Toni snarled.

Imogen's shout of laughter sounded close to hysteria. 'Actually, he's police. You picked the wrong time to chase me.'

Toni's face grew pale. Reality sinking in, perhaps.

Adam would let the deception stand.

They drove to the village, Adam leading the way, slowly. There had been enough *Top Gear* heroics for one day. They parked in The Plough's car park and trooped in single file to Adam's private entrance.

Pans clattered in the kitchen. Adam closed the linking door. 'Right, then. Let's hear it all.'

Toni had gathered her wits. 'I'm sorry. I didn't mean to frighten you. I saw you driving out of the police station and followed. It was a spur-of-the-moment thing.'

'Like last time? A bit of a coincidence, isn't it? You bump into me every time I visit the station.'

Adam voiced a thought. 'Someone tipping you off, are they? A friend in the station?'

The flush deepened. 'Well,' Toni's gaze ricocheted between Adam and Imogen. 'You see – I know someone who works there, and he just happened to mention it.'

'Then it's a good job I'm retired, or your friend would be in serious trouble.'

Toni gulped. 'It's my son, actually.' Her eyes pleaded. 'Please, don't tell anyone. I know he shouldn't have told me – he said no, at first, but I kept on at him until he agreed—'

Imogen interrupted, acid in her voice, 'And you're his mother. He didn't want to let you down.'

Toni didn't react to the sarcasm. 'He's worked hard to get

where he is. He only did it to help me. I heard about Greg's death, and I mentioned to Stephen – my son – that I'd been planning to invite you to the reunion, so he texted me when he saw you in the station – he'd seen your photo in the station as a...' she stopped.

'As a suspect in my husband's murder? Thanks, Toni. So much for old friends. Why didn't you just come to the hotel? It's not difficult to find.' She jerked a thumb in the vague direction of the hotel across the lane.

'I didn't know you'd come back – I mean, you and your father never got on, even at school.'

The woman's story made sense. Maybe she had just wanted to find Imogen and enjoyed speeding through the countryside.

While Imogen digested Toni's story, Adam seized his chance. 'When did you last see Gregory Bishop?' That made her jump!

'What? Are you suggesting...?'

'I'm not suggesting anything. It's a simple question. You knew him, he was an old friend.'

Toni folded her arms. 'I haven't seen him for years. I've been away – I only came back recently, to sort out a care home for my father.'

'You've been in touch with the others.' Imogen pointed out. 'All our friends from school – Steph and Kate, and Daniel, too, not to mention Mrs Hall.

Toni nodded. 'We met up to plan the evening. The four of us and Mrs Hall. We thought it was time to... to lay the ghost, I suppose. It's always haunted us.'

'Me too,' Imogen acknowledged. 'None of us were covered in glory, that night.'

Toni shrugged. 'It was Julian's own fault. He drank too much, fell over and hit his head.'

Imogen exchanged a glance with Adam. Either Toni truly

thought the death was an accident, or she was covering up the truth.

They sent her on her way, and stood by the window in the bar, watching as the SUV negotiated the road from the village with exquisite care.

'We're no further forward, are we?' Imogen commented. 'We still don't know why she was following me.'

Time for a warning. 'You need to take care. One of your old acquaintances is no real friend. We don't know which, and if they've killed three times, they won't hesitate to do it again.'

'Toni, Steph, Kate and Daniel. All in the tunnel that day, and all back now. How do we narrow it down?'

'We need the motive. Opportunity's there for all of them and method: a bang on the head for Julian, debris on the road for your father, and poison for Greg.'

Imogen's frown lifted. 'Isn't poison a woman's weapon?'

Adam saw the hope on her face. She didn't want it to be Daniel. He sighed, about to spoil the moment. 'Never heard of Dr Crippen?'

34

PAINTER

Steph Aldred appeared on Adam's doorstep the next day. Dressed in a multicoloured jacket, dark hair tousled by a sharp spring breeze, she brought a smile to his lips.

'I'm so sorry to bother you,' she said. 'Is it too inconvenient?'

'Not at all. Come in.'

She stood in the middle of the room, twisting a chunky bracelet round her wrist, refusing coffee or tea, or even to sit down. 'You surprised me at home,' she said, 'and I was rude. You were a policeman and I don't like people checking up on me.'

'Not at all unusual.'

Smiling, she examined the room. 'This is not what I would expect for a police officer. It's enchanting. And you own the pub as well?'

'That's retirement for you. I'm just an amateur painter and pub landlord, now.'

'That sounds like fun – hard work, though, I should think.'

What had she really come to say? He waited. She'd get there in her own time.

Sure enough, she took a deep breath. 'You asked me about

Greg, and when I last saw him. Oh,' she held up a hand, as if in self-defence, 'I didn't exactly lie to you. But I didn't tell you every-thing I knew. I didn't tell you about that time at school.'

'I'd like to hear it from your point of view.'

'It's hard to remember details, after all this time.'

'The parts you recall may be different to your friends' memo-ries. It all adds to the picture.'

Eyes bright with intelligence, Steph considered. 'You think our stupid escapade may have something to do with Greg's death?'

'Who knows? They may be linked – or not. Why don't you sit down? I want to hear anything you can tell me. Your friend, Imogen, is under suspicion for her husband's murder and she's frightened, although she hides it well. You were her friend. Your memories may help.'

She backed into a chair and Adam bustled about with coffee. 'That school reunion. What a weird evening. It had seemed like a good idea, at first.'

'Who's idea?'

Her eyes slid away. 'It just grew. I met Mrs Hall in Camilton, and we talked about it then. Poor old soul. You'd think she'd had enough of school, at her age, but she never married. Maybe she thinks of us all as her children. Some people have cats, Mrs Hall has old pupils.' She laughed. 'That sounds too fanciful for words.'

'Not necessarily. Go on.' He handed over a mug of coffee.

'Once we'd agreed to go ahead, we rounded up everyone we could find. Daniel had moved back – another one of us with a broken marriage – and he was really keen. He kept asking if Imogen would be there.'

She gazed into her coffee mug. 'We were so pleased to see her, although she left early. A bit overcome, I think, so soon after

Greg's death. Seeing us all there again, Greg's friends, must have been very difficult.'

She seemed to have dried up. He tried an encouraging nod.

'Before, I told you I didn't like Greg.'

'But?'

'That wasn't quite true. We all fancied Greg like mad.'

'Greg, not Daniel?'

She shook her head. 'We hardly knew Daniel was there in those days. He sort of lurked in the background, watching. Something to do with being a painter, perhaps? Looking on, rather than joining in. Oh,' she grinned. 'You're a painter, too.'

'Not in Daniel's league, I'm afraid.'

'He's talented, isn't he? But, in those days, we all wanted Greg.'

'All the girls liked him?'

She nodded. 'And he knew it. He went out with all of us, one by one. More than just "going out", really.' Her eyes stayed fixed on the window. 'If you see what I mean.'

'You mean, he took advantage of the girls?'

'If they let him. His friends called him "The Ram".'

'Which girls?' Adam asked, his voice gentle.

'Not me. He didn't take much notice of me.' Was that resentment in her voice? 'Toni first. They were together for nearly a year, and then they broke up, and he was with Kate for a while, but all the time, it was Imogen he really liked. You could tell. He was always beside her. She was different from the rest of us. Very tall, very self-contained, with all that beautiful hair. She looked like a Greek goddess,'

Would Imogen recognise that description?

'The thing is...' Steph said. 'When Toni left school, she took a year out before university. She moved away from Camilton and out of Somerset altogether. I didn't really notice, because we no longer saw each other – only Kate and Toni kept in touch – but when we were at the reunion, we talked about our children. None of us had a very good record with husbands, but we all had children – except for Imogen.'

Adam sat up, listening hard.

'I have my daughter, Rose, and Toni has Stephen, who's a policeman. Imogen went home early, and we dragged out our old photos. They were in our handbags – nobody wanted to show them off while Imogen was there. There's nothing worse than other people's children if you don't have one of your own.'

Adam didn't have children. Did she know?

'You can imagine us, can't you, lining up the photos on a table, all thinking our own kids were the best looking.' She laughed. 'There was one of Stephen with some friends. And, one of those friends, a bit older than Stephen, looked just like Greg. He had the same sort of crinkly hair and broad shoulders.' She paused.

Adam held his breath. She was about to say something dramatic.

'It turned out that boy was Kate's son. And he was just the right age to be born the year we left school.'

'You mean...'

'I think Greg got Kate pregnant.'

The silence stretched out. Adam thought hard.

What of Imogen? She had no child, but her husband did. She didn't see the photos – maybe she didn't know. Or perhaps his child was the reason for their quarrel and the end of their marriage?

Or was Steph leading Adam up the garden path? Deflecting suspicion from herself, or from another friend?

So many questions to answer.

'My darling Adam.' Maria's head appeared round the doorway. 'Let me in. You're late for—' She broke off. 'Steph? What are you doing here?' It took her a moment to recover. 'Steph, darling,

I didn't know you two were friends. Adam, you should have told me. Steph is a dear friend.' She clasped the smaller woman to her bosom. 'Steph is our newest addition to the orchestra. She plays the flute. Oh, you will love our concert.'

Steph untangled herself and backed towards the door. 'I'll see myself out.'

Maria narrowed her eyes. 'Adam, is Steph Aldred one of your girlfriends?'

'I'm too old for girlfriends.' He forced a smile. No need to be testy. 'Tell me. What can I help you with today?'

'But surely you can't have forgotten? We have a meeting of the Concert Committee. The concert is just two days away. And you are late for the meeting. Mrs Bishop sent me to find you.'

* * *

Emily and Imogen were waiting in the office, while Harley lay curled contentedly in his basket under the receptionist's desk.

Maria's plans for the concert had expanded. It promised to be the biggest social event of the year.

Emily kept the worst of her nonsense within bounds, steering the conversation successfully from caviar and champagne to cheese and wine, 'People will come for the Mozart, not the food.' And to see where the mysterious murder took place.

They spent an hour running through plans. Tickets were selling like hot cakes and most of the village would be there. It would be an evening to remember.

Maria left, kissing everyone on both cheeks. Emily returned to her duties and Adam suggested a walk with Imogen and Harley. The dog lifted one ear, jumped up and bounded to the door.

Imogen clipped on the animal's lead and they set off for the village.

Adam's anger overflowed. 'When will you be honest with me?'

'Sorry? What?' His fierceness seemed to startle her.

'Why didn't you tell me about Greg's son? Surely, you knew about him?'

'Oh.'

'Is that all you can say? Oh? You knew, didn't you?'

Her eyes opened in shock – or a display of innocence? He wasn't about to be fooled.

'Your dead husband fathered a child by one of your friends, and you didn't bother to mention it?'

'Well, I...'

'We're supposed to be partners, but you're keeping me in the dark. Don't you see how guilty you look? Greg and Kate had a son together, and you didn't bother to tell me? What am I supposed to think?'

Imogen had turned her face away.

'I'm sorry,' she whispered. 'I didn't think Greg's son had anything to do with his death.'

'You didn't? Well, sooner or later, DCI Andrews is going to find out, and then he'll have a great big motive that will convince him to charge you with murder. And I wouldn't blame him.'

They rounded the corner to the scene of Alfie Croft's bicycle crash. So many accidents, so many loose ends. Adam's head swam a little.

Imogen had turned deathly pale.

'Tell me about it.'

'I didn't know about the boy for years. I can't have children, you see.' She shrugged. 'I had all the tests. I really wanted a family. I was ready to start IVF, but Greg wouldn't do it. We fought about it all the time. Then, one day, he told me he didn't need more children, because he already had one.'

The bleakness in her voice chilled Adam.

She choked on a sob. 'Greg really wasn't a very nice person.'

He offered a handkerchief. She blew her nose.

'Nobody carries handkerchiefs.'

'I'm old-school.'

She offered a watery smile.

'Did you know Kate was the mother?' Adam asked.

'Oh, yes. Greg enjoyed telling me that. He said he would have married her, but he was too young to be a father. So he married me instead.'

Adam said, 'Do you know, I think your husband deserved everything he got. I'm just surprised no one killed him sooner.'

'I thought about it, once or twice. You know, in a sort of dreamy way. What would it be like to get rid of him? But we rubbed along together most of the time. He could be fun, when he wanted to. And I'd married him of my own free will. No one forced me to.'

'Although he wasn't your real choice?'

'How did you guess?' She sniffed. 'It was Daniel I wanted. I always liked Daniel, but he didn't take much notice of me at school. It was different when he came to paint the garden. At least, at first – then he just... disappeared. When Greg asked me out, I was flattered. The other girls were jealous.' She offered Adam his handkerchief, now screwed into a damp ball.

'No thanks. It's a present.'

'Another present? You already gave me Harley. What can I give you in return?'

'Honesty?'

She laughed, almost back to normal. 'Full disclosure, then. When Daniel was painting the garden, we grew close. I was engaged to Greg, but I would have left him in a moment if Daniel asked me to. Instead, he disappeared, overnight, without even saying goodbye.' She dabbed at her eyes again. 'He broke my heart. All I could do was pretend I didn't care, and marry Greg. I've sometimes suspected Greg knew how I felt – that I was in love with Daniel. My father said Daniel was a loser, but he liked Greg.'

'Any idea why?'

She took a moment to answer. 'They had so much in common with their various business interests. They liked secrets – knowing things that I didn't, putting one over on me.' She picked leaves from a nearby Daphne bush, shredding them between her fingers. 'I couldn't wait to marry and move away from home, permanently. My mother was already dead and Dad had his series of women.' The colour had come back in her cheeks. 'I can see why the police would think it, but I really didn't kill Greg. Or anyone else.'

'Who do you think did, then?'

There was a long pause. 'I don't know. I mean – I don't want to jump to conclusions, but I'm almost sure it was one of us. From school. I just don't know who.'

Adam gave her a long look. 'When you say you don't want to jump to conclusions, do you mean you have an idea?'

'Just that – an idea. And I think I know how to find out for sure.'

Adam took her arm and turned her to face him. 'Imogen, don't put yourself in harm's way. There's a murderer out there.'

'It's OK. I can look after myself. Now, let's give Harley a proper run.'

35

BOTTLE

Harley was still full of energy, so instead of going indoors, Imogen took him into the garden. It had turned, unexpectedly, into a beautiful afternoon, with clear skies, hardly any breeze, and a warm sun. Imogen took a short path that wound behind a row of apple trees. The blossom had gone, and tiny fruits were beginning to set.

'Summer's coming, Harley.' She let him off the lead to run while she tugged weeds from a bed of peonies. The blooms would burst soon, with a glorious few days of exquisite blowsiness, followed by months of inaction. The laziest plants in the garden, her father had called them, and the most beautiful.

Oswald arrived, standing like a ghost beside her. 'I've done what you asked, ma'am,' he said, with a peculiar gesture halfway between a salute and a tug of his forelock. Imogen often thought he should have lived a hundred years ago. 'I planted a few nasturtiums and jasmine by the orangery. They'll grow fast, cover the place in months, I shouldn't wonder.'

'I saw, thank you. And, it's the wrong time of year to plant trees, but maybe a few larger bushes?' To hide it further from gawping guests and put off, a little longer, the inevitable decision about the building's future.

'Yes, ma'am. Then, come the winter, we'll put in some proper broad leaved specimens. Make a little woodland round here.'

'That would be nice.'

Something nagged at the back of Imogen's mind, but the thought was misty. Was it something she'd heard, or seen?

She thought about the reunion. That ghastly evening had brought the ill-fated picnic into glaring focus – the same people there, the teenage friendships with their underlying tensions, the unbearable outcome...

Her heart raced. There was something wrong – something that didn't fit. Other people's memories of that day didn't add up. If only her mind would clear she'd grasp it.

Oswald cleared his throat.

The misty thought evaporated. 'Sorry. I was miles away. What do you need?'

'I wanted to tell you I cleaned up the orangery yesterday.'

'What do you mean?' She didn't need this other image – the sight of Greg's dead body – in her head. She wanted to remember him from the early years of their marriage, when she'd thought they were happy.

Oswald leaned on his spade. 'After... you know. Your husband, rest his soul.' He coughed and started again. 'Once the police took their tape away, we left the place alone. Gave me the shivers, to be honest. But I went in, thinking it was time to tidy up.' He cleared his throat.

Bless the man, he'd gone in to check there were no signs of Greg's death left to upset her.

'I found a couple of empty bottles that hadn't been there before.'

'Bottles? How did they get there?'

He pulled the spade from the ground and stabbed at a deep-rooted weed. 'Someone went there after the police left. Hotel guests, I suppose.'

'Guests shouldn't be coming to the orangery. It's fenced off.'

'Easy enough to climb over a bit of fence.'

True enough. Children did it every summer, scrumping apples from farms.

'When did it happen?' She hadn't been able to face the orangery.

'Ah, now you're asking.' Oswald screwed his face up until his eyes threatened to disappear altogether and scratched the back of his head. 'No, sorry, Miss Imogen. One day's like another to me. Could have been any time.'

'Was there much damage?'

'Nothing deliberate, I reckon; a couple of empty beer bottles and some broken glass in the plant pots. Boys from the village larking about, if you ask me.' He sucked his teeth. 'Those young lads – no respect.'

'Mm.' She hadn't seen young lads around lately. A shiver crawled up Imogen's spine. 'I expect you're right, it was lads from the village on a night out. Keep a lookout, will you, Oswald? We don't want it to become a habit.'

Oswald attacked the dandelions while Imogen headed for the orangery. *I bet those bottles appeared the night the earring arrived.* Who had left them: lads on a night out, a member of the hotel staff or someone from her past?

Harley sat at her feet. The sun warmed her back; rosemary and lavender scented the air in the garden. Absently, she rubbed Harley's chest until he fell asleep, snoring gently. Still, she sat, thinking, piecing together clues. There were so many; too many. If only she could see clearly.

She had no idea how long she sat, thinking, until the pieces of the jigsaw began to fall into place.

Harley opened one eye as she stood. 'I wonder if I'm right, Harley. At least, I know how to find out.'

The dog licked her outstretched fingers.

'The concert at the weekend. That's when I'll know.'

The day of Maria's concert dawned at last. The preparations were complete, chairs set out on the hotel lawn, a dais for the orchestra erected and covered against the rain, refreshments under preparation.

Emily had whirled through the hotel like a dervish yesterday, checking arrangements.

Imogen squinted at the sky. 'At least the weather's fine so far.'

She tried to breathe slowly, fighting an attack of nervous excitement. Today's plans reached far beyond hosting a village event.

Her phone trilled. Emily sounded uncharacteristically panicky. 'Michael's called in sick.'

One of the serving staff, he'd agreed to pick up the star tenor from Cardiff. The man would now be arriving at the railway station in Camilton at midday, ready for final rehearsals.

'Don't worry,' Imogen said, soothingly. 'If there's no one else around, I'll collect him. Everything's under control.' Funny, to hear Emily in a state over something so simple.

That call was the first of many. Cool, calm members of staff had taken leave of their senses, struggling with the simplest decision.

Imogen hid her turmoil with a display of calm. Tonight, she would find out if her worst fears were realised.

She checked the list of ticket holders. Everyone she wanted to be there had bought a ticket. So long as they all arrived...

She immersed herself in the final details.

She hadn't anticipated such enthusiasm for Mozart among the staff. Everyone planned to be there tonight, whether on duty or not. She'd even heard the youngest waitress humming excerpts from *The Marriage of Figaro* in the kitchens.

Harley, picking up the mood of tension and expectation, galloped in overexcited circles in the foyer until Imogen banished him to her rooms for the morning. 'The last thing we need is a guest tripping over and breaking a leg.'

Halfway down the main stairs, she stopped. The walls were covered with photos of VIPs shaking hands with her father. A lump formed in Imogen's throat. How he would have loved tonight's event.

Sentimentality flew out of the window when the old grandfather clock chimed ten. Time for the daily staff meeting.

Breaking crockery crashed in the dining room. Someone shrieked. Imogen put her head round the door.

'I'm so sorry, Mrs Bishop.' The tiny waitress's face crumpled. 'They slipped out of my hands.'

'Never mind. Clear it up and join the meeting.'

She looked at the row of staff faces, all scrubbed and fresh. Anticipation electrified the air.

She cleared her throat and summoned the spirit of her father. 'I want to thank you all for your hard work. It hasn't been easy at The Streamside Hotel recently.'

She looked into each face. Many nodded.

'My father would be proud of the way you've all worked together. The hotel looks wonderful. The bunting around the front is a triumph.'

She hated bunting, but the staff had begged.

'Now, some things are bound to go wrong today, no matter how carefully we've planned.'

The butterfingered waitress blushed scarlet.

'Whatever happens, you'll cope, and the evening will be a roaring success. Just remember that our job is to make sure everyone enjoys themselves – sensibly.'

They laughed. The barmen, army veterans who'd been in Afghanistan, flexed their muscles.

'We'll be busy, but I hope you'll all enjoy the music, even if you're at the other end of the hotel. Emily and I will be here all day. Bring any problems you can't manage to us – any you can't solve with ingenuity and common sense, I mean.'

Another ripple of laughter.

She decided to stop while she was winning. 'Have a wonderful day.'

The round of applause took her by surprise.

'I didn't know you were such a competent public speaker.' Adam had arrived, unseen. 'Now, are you sure this is going to work?'

He didn't mean the concert.

'Everything will be fine. Stop worrying.'

* * *

The day passed in a whirl of activity. Adam offered to collect the celebrity tenor from the station.

'Never again,' he grumbled. 'The man "warmed up the voice" all the way, right in my ear.'

By the time Imogen released Harley from quarantine in her room, the select group of VIPs had finished their pre-concert meals and were gathered in the lounge.

Maria held court, surrounded by local men. 'Yes, I arranged this evening, although Mr Hennessy helped. Oh,' she caught sight of Imogen. 'Mrs Bishop has so kindly offered the hotel as a venue. We thought to use the garden of The Plough – such lovely views to Ham Hill – but there was something about licences...'

Imogen hurried outside as, from all over Somerset, the rest of the audience arrived, dressed in their best evening clothes, carrying wicker baskets and rugs, ready to picnic in the hotel grounds.

'Almost as charming as Glyndebourne,' announced Jonathan Hampton.

Helen Pickles and her mild-mannered accountant husband talked ghoulish shop with Adam's pathologist friend.

'Bodies fished out of the River Parrett are the worst,' James explained.

Imogen hurried past, took a deep breath, straightened her emerald green dress, checked no wayward strands of hair had escaped their moorings, and greeted her special guests.

Steph arrived, alone. No Daniel? They were a couple, weren't they?

Toni and Kate arrived together with Mrs Hall.

Imogen chatted about the weather, trying to sound relaxed, but her nerves jangled. Would he come?

The owner of Haselbury House stood with the Jenkins and Hamptons, reliving last year's pheasant shoot.

Councillor Smith and the mayor gushed over Imogen with reminiscences of her father.

Daniel appeared, looking sensational in evening dress. Imogen counted to ten and greeted him with a demure handshake, afraid he might hear the pounding of her heart. She longed to stay, catch up with him, talk over old times, but there was no time.

At the very last moment, her final guest appeared.

She glanced across at Adam, their eyes met, and she nodded.

Everything was falling into place. The stage was set.

* * *

The chattering parties broke up, the audience finding their seats as the time arrived for the concert to begin. Adam sank down next to Imogen at the back of the lawn.

Maria stepped forward. Spectacular in an ice-blue column dress that showed off every scintillating curve, she enjoyed every second of her time in the spotlight. She thanked the audience for coming, her charming accent only a little exaggerated, and swept into her seat in the front row of the choir.

Adam's mouth was half open. Imogen nudged him and he closed it with a snap.

At last, the concert began.

The conductor bounded to the music stand, beamed at the audience, smiled at the orchestra, glared at the bass player scrabbling on the floor for a sheet of missing music, and tapped his baton.

Even Adam enjoyed the cheerful excerpts from Mozart operas and Strauss waltzes. He whispered, 'If only the fat lady wouldn't sing.'

Imogen shushed him.

He checked his watch, counting down the minutes. Would their plan work?

Right on cue, a convoy of cars drew up, engines roaring, shattering the silence that fell at the end of the first half.

Their timing was perfect.

The audience turned as one to watch Chief Inspector Andrews stroll to the dais.

The conductor blinked, lost for words, and backed away.

The DCI asked everyone to remain seated. Uniformed officers arranged themselves behind the audience, faces expressionless, eyes roaming ceaselessly across the rows.

'I'm sorry to interrupt your evening, ladies and gentlemen, but a serious crime has been committed,' DCI Andrews announced.

A murmur rose from the audience.

Councillor Smith half rose, thought better of it, and subsided.

The DCI continued. 'My colleague, Adam Hennessy, will tell you more.'

Adam made his way to the front and took a moment to scan the rows of puzzled faces. 'As some of you know, I was a detective with the Birmingham police,' he began, in a conversational tone. 'I retired last year, after a long and difficult case. Several members of a local gang were arrested and charged as a result of that case and their trials are due to begin very soon.'

The audience murmured, restless.

'You're wondering what that has to do with Lower Hembrow, or with any part of Somerset. Be patient, and I'll explain.' He leaned on the music stand. 'This gang, mostly Cypriots, made alliances with criminals across the West Midlands and the South West of England. Many of their allies are not, on the face of it, thugs or bandits.'

The memory of his dead cat, its blood soaked into the rug on his living room floor, flashed into his head, and for a second, he lost his thread.

He recovered quickly. 'It pains me, very much, to tell you that the previous owner of this hotel was involved with some of their fraudulent activities.'

Several of the audience gasped.

'Some of his activities were illegal, while others were charitable and designed to benefit this community, one he loved.'

Here and there, a head nodded agreement.

'Detective Chief Inspector Andrews has been investigation Councillor Jones' death and he's come to a disturbing conclusion.'

Adam's eyes sought Imogen in the back row.

Satisfied by her tentative smile, he dropped the bombshell. 'Councillor Jones' car crash was not, as previously thought, an unexpected accident.'

More gasps.

'No, I'm afraid the councillor was the victim of a particularly devious and unpleasant killer.' He looked round the audience. 'One of you here today was responsible. DCI Andrews and his men wish to question several members of this audience.' He swept his hand in an arc, encompassing the rows of wide-eyed spectators. 'Police officers will take your names, whereupon those of you not needed will be free to leave.' He ended, 'I apologise for spoiling this evening's event.'

An excited babble began, slowly at first, building, and rising to a climax as police blocked the row where Councillor Smith and the mayor sat, shock contorting their features.

Adam tapped the music stand and the babble died. 'By the way, we have an important clue.' He held up the pearl earring in a white-gloved hand. It glinted in the orange glow of the evening sun. 'This is a piece of valuable evidence. Our forensic team,' he nodded towards James, who stood to offer a ridiculous little bow, 'have undertaken many tests that yielded vital information. This earring was found in the grounds of this very hotel, near to where

Mr Gregory Bishop died. The police will be grateful for any information as to how it found its way there.'

If the police had not been in attendance, there would have been bedlam in the hotel garden. DCI Andrews' officers kept the situation under control, standing at the ends of the rows of seats, holding clipboards, organising an orderly exodus, and taking names.

The audience, far more excited than dismayed at the sudden end of their evening's entertainment, filed obediently past and gathered in chattering groups. A series of gasps put an end to the conversation.

A silence fell, as the entire audience turned to watch the mayor and Councillor Smith, their heads lowered, eyes averted, escorted from the garden into one of the police cars and driven away.

At the back of the audience, Imogen's eyes remained fixed on her old school friends.

37

DAVID

The police finally persuaded most of the audience to go home, but Imogen's friends remained, in a tight huddle.

She studied their expressions, searching for clues. Who had recognised the earring? Their faces gave little away.

'Well, that was spectacular,' Steph said.

Adam took a position next to Imogen.

Daniel looked from one to the other. 'What happens now? None of us know anything about this earring, or Greg's death, so I suppose we can all go home?'

He made to move away, but James, bulky and grinning, enjoying every moment of the evening, blocked his path. 'Not so fast. Adam and Imogen have something to say.'

'Something else?' Toni sniggered. 'Haven't you had enough of the limelight?'

Adam said, 'I think you should all come inside if you want to know who killed Gregory Bishop.'

'Of course, we want to know.' Steph sounded indignant.

'Well, listen and learn.'

Imogen ushered them all into the empty lounge. They sat, silent, in a circle, watching Adam, but it was Imogen who spoke.

'There's one more person here who's keen to join us. None of you recognised him when he arrived, because it's a long time since you've met. Here he is...'

A tall, slim figure in horn-rimmed glasses appeared from the dining room, where he'd sat out the evening, waiting for Imogen's signal.

Steph broke the puzzled silence. 'I know who you are. You're David. David Canberra.'

The others muttered to each other, but Daniel stood up and held out a hand, surprising them all. 'David. It's been a long time.'

Kate said, 'What are you doing here?'

The new arrival ducked his head, looking nervous, and took Daniel's outstretched hand. 'Good to see you all again,' he said. 'Imogen tracked me down.'

'It wasn't hard. Canberra's not a common name in Cornwall.'

David slid into a chair.

Adam handed round cups of coffee, but most of the group waved it away, their eyes fixed firmly on Imogen.

She took a deep breath and began. 'One of you already knows everything I'm about to tell you, but the rest have no idea. I'm going to take you all back to the evening in the tunnel under our school – the picnic we've all tried so hard to forget.'

Her gaze roamed around the room, but no one seemed willing to meet her eyes.

'We kept away from each other after we left school. Not surprising, was it? Julian had died, and we all felt terrible. At least, I know I did.' She sighed, wishing she didn't have to continue. 'I have a confession to make. An act of cruelty that I've bitterly regretted for all these years. You see, that night in the tunnel, Julian asked me out.'

No one spoke.

'Instead of thanking him for the compliment, selfish beast that I was, I laughed at him.' There, it was out. Would they all hate her?

To her surprise, no one moved.

She turned to David. 'You were his friend, and you were watching. You saw it, didn't you?'

'I did.' David's expression was unreadable.

Several people shifted in their chairs.

Toni stood up, pointing at David. 'You pushed Julian. We all know that. You had a stand-up fight and he fell over, hit his head, and died.'

Imogen waved at her to sit. 'That's the story, but is it true? How did you hear it? Hearsay? Rumour? Some of the gossip you love so much?'

Toni glowered and sat down, her mouth clamped shut.

Imogen continued, 'David has a different story to tell.'

She heard a sharp intake of breath.

'Of course, he does.' Kate said, scornfully. 'He killed his friend. He won't admit that.'

Imogen ignored the interruption. 'Julian's death was no more an accident than that of my father.'

'Nonsense.' This time, Steph leapt up. 'You can't believe that. Why would anyone kill Julian? He was so... so harmless.'

Adam intervened. 'Let Imogen speak.'

'Motive,' Imogen said. 'That was one of the problems facing us, as Adam and I puzzled over Julian's death. It's been so long since he died that the truth was hidden under layers of confusion. You're quite right, Steph. At first sight, no one had any reason to hurt him; we were so self-absorbed, we hardly noticed when he was around. The same was true with you, I'm afraid.' She smiled an apology at David.

'I'm over it,' he said. 'I was never memorable. It used to hurt, but now I'm happily married with three grown children, it seems so far in the past. If we'd known how things would turn out, it would have saved so much teenage angst.'

'If only,' Imogen agreed, from her heart. 'Here we are, all these years later, with all those teenage anxieties and jealousies in the past. It seems to me David is about the only one of us who's been truly successful.' She flicked a hand in the air. 'I don't mean, successful in business. I mean, in life.'

Daniel spoke, slowly, as though thinking his words through, 'Do you think the events of that night may have something to do with our disappointing lives? Look at us – mostly divorced, avoiding each other, shutting ourselves into our own prisons. The burden we've carried, all these years – Julian's tragic death and our parts in it – has cast a shadow over everything we've done.'

Steph said, 'Or, perhaps we're just losers. We can't blame Julian for the mess we've made of our own lives.'

Imogen admired Steph's blunt honesty. She'd always been like that. Telling the truth had led to her expulsion from school. She'd confessed to drinking and taking LSD that night, while the rest of them had lied, insisting they'd had soft drinks and didn't know they'd been spiked.

But one awkward fact remained – her earring had appeared beside the orangery.

'This is all very well,' Steph said, 'but you haven't answered the big question. Why would anyone kill Julian?'

'I'll come to that in a moment.' Imogen paused, keeping her thoughts in order. 'As you'll know from tonight's events—'

'And, wasn't that quite a show?' Toni, recovered from her minor humiliation, joined in again, holding out her cup for a refill, leaning back against the squashy cushions of her armchair.

Adam spoke up. 'Effective, I'd say. All the players in one place.'

Imogen raised her voice. 'Before we tell you our conclusions, I'd like to talk about my husband. You see, his murder is connected to Julian's.' She looked around their shocked faces. 'Indulge me a moment. Why would anyone want to kill Greg? True, he was never a dream husband. I knew he was unfaithful – that was why I wouldn't take him back after he left – but there was one thing I didn't know, and it's important. Some of you are already aware of this.'

She forced her hands to lie still in her lap, as long pent-up fury threatened to explode.

'Greg had a child.'

From the corner of her eyes, she saw Kate's leg twitch. 'Yes, Kate. He never told me and nor did you – and I thought you were my best friend.'

38

Discussing Greg's son had taken all Imogen's strength.

She stopped talking and slumped in her chair, eyes closed, as Adam took over. 'Leaving the past aside for a moment, and the parentage of Greg's son, let's jump forward to your reunion. There seemed to be no connection between Greg's death and the reunion. But then, this earring appeared near the murder scene. The last time Imogen saw it was at the reunion.'

Steph held up a hand. 'OK, I'll confess. That's my earring. When you showed it today, I was too shocked to admit it was mine, but I don't see that it matters. I've no idea how it came to be in Imogen's hotel garden.'

Imogen opened her eyes. Adam's smile was sad. 'Just one of the mysteries associated with this case. One of the problems has been, not lack of clues, but an overabundance of them. Clues have popped up everywhere we looked. Enough for a treasure hunt, and most of them planted deliberately to point the finger anywhere except towards the killer. Greg's body was left in Imogen's back garden. Was that designed to put her under suspicion? Steph's earring was planted in the same garden. Was that so she'd come under suspicion, or did she plant it herself, to muddy the waters – a kind of double bluff?'

He smiled. 'The hotel garden is important to this investigation. Greg died from poison – rat poison, used routinely in the hotel garden and kept in the potting shed. Another pointer towards Imogen, or perhaps a member of staff at the hotel? It's the same back garden,' he looked straight at Daniel, 'where you discovered the councillor's involvement in the theft of rare plants.'

Daniel sounded confused. 'All I did was paint them, and I lost the job as a result. I know nothing about this earring.' Tears sprang to Imogen's eyes as he added, 'I can't imagine why anyone would think Imogen capable of killing anyone.'

'On the contrary,' Adam interrupted, 'I believe any of us could kill if we had strong enough reasons, but let's stick to the evidence. Imogen and I have sifted through leads, false leads, and misdirection. So, instead of following clues that we came to realise had been planted, we came back to motive. Any one of you had the opportunity to kill each of these three people, and probably could find the means – but why should you want to? That's the key.' He held up a hand. 'Let's look at possible reasons for killing the councillor. There are plenty.'

He ticked them off on his fingers. 'One. He was involved with various crimes. Never doing the dirty work himself, always on the periphery, but raking in the money. The police will find it in some hidden account; they've been tracing his affairs. He was being blackmailed by an old friend on the town council.

'Second, he'd sacked you, Daniel, and set your career back by years.'

'But I didn't kill him, no matter how you twist things. I've managed just fine since then.' Daniel's expression hardened and tension crackled between the two.

Adam cracked a reluctant smile. 'True enough, and I agree. You didn't kill the councillor, not because you never would, but because you have no motive to murder Julian or Greg. Try as I might, I couldn't find one, and there's only one killer here.

'Let's look at motive for killing Greg, then.' Adam touched a third finger. 'He cheated three of you. Toni, by dropping you and moving on to Kate. Kate, by fathering your child and marrying Imogen, and Imogen, by keeping his child a secret.'

He waited.

'All three of you had motives for killing Greg, out of jealousy. That narrowed the field a little. Imogen had sent Greg packing, glad to see the back of him. Why would she kill him? He wasn't rich, although he'd emptied their bank account. Even the police have realised she had nothing to gain from his death, or that of Julian. Once again, a motive for one death, that of her father, but not the others. We can clear Imogen.' He looked at Steph. 'Apart from keeping quiet about the earring, and having a hand in organising the reunion, you had no motive for any of the three murders. You're off the hook, too.

'So, we're left with Toni and Kate. Imogen's old school friends. Friends, who both had reason to hate her. She was always in the way, wasn't she? The boys liked her, even shy little Julian. Greg wanted to marry her, and Daniel admired her from a distance.'

Imogen put in, 'Toni, you risked your son's career, asking him to tell you when I was in the police station. Did you really hate me that much?'

Adam interrupted. 'Maybe she did. You married Greg, the boy she wanted, but that was no reason for her to kill him. They hadn't even met for years.' He glared at Toni. 'You weren't off the hook entirely, until we discovered someone else with more reason to hate Imogen.'

He waited, as everyone in the room slowly turned towards

Kate. Adam spoke to her directly. 'Recently, you renewed your affair with Greg.'

Colour drained from Kate's face. 'Nonsense,' she snapped.

Adam said, 'Not nonsense at all. Oswald, the gardener at the hotel, saw you together one day. Only, he was confused – he thought you were Emily, the hotel manager, and inadvertently threw us off your trail. It was an easy mistake to make – you look a little alike, especially to an old man with fading eyesight. You're both small, with neat blonde hair, cut in a similar style.'

Kate's hands flew to her head, as though trying to cover her hair.

'You met Greg in the orangery, away from prying eyes. Unfortunately for you, you took things too far – planted too much evidence and told too many lies.'

39

Livid purple suffused Kate's face. Her eyes, dark with hate, bored into Imogen. 'You were always the special one, weren't you? Clever, your father a big shot in town, Greg fawning all over you when he was supposed to be with me – and even Julian wanted you.'

Kate jumped to her feet, kicked over the coffee table, sending cups flying, coffee splashing the carpet, and made a dash for the French doors.

David got there first. He slammed his hands against the glass. 'I don't think so,' he said, in a conversational tone. 'You're not getting away. You murdered my best friend; Julian was the kindest, brightest person I knew, and you killed him.' He ground his teeth. 'If you weren't a woman...'

'That's enough, sir.' DCI Andrews came in from the foyer. 'We'll deal with the lady.'

The young constable followed him in, marched across the room and took Kate's arm in a firm grip. 'No need for a fuss, ma'am.'

Kate's gaze flew around the room, searching, but there was no escape.

David returned to his seat, his lips white with anger, his hands still clenched into fists.

Adam asked, 'Who invited Julian to the picnic that night?'

David said, 'Kate. She told me she fancied him and got me to bring him along.'

'And you noticed something that didn't seem to matter at the time...'

David nodded. 'She had a hammer in her bag. I saw it when we were trying to break through the end of the tunnel. It was blocked up and she said, "I thought this might happen." We took it in turns to attack the wall with the hammer, but we didn't hit too hard – we didn't want to cause so much damage the staff would investigate. After a few taps, we saw the wall was solid, so we stopped trying. I didn't notice what happened to the hammer. I suppose she dropped it back in her bag.'

He took off his glasses and polished them. 'When we left the tunnel, we were all pretty woozy from the drinks. Julian dropped behind us all. I could see he was upset because Imogen had turned him down. He blew his nose, like he was crying or something, so I pretended I hadn't noticed and left him behind – didn't want to embarrass him. Kate was beside him and I thought she'd cheer him up. I bought the whole "accident" idea, but looking back, I'm sure she hit him. It never occurred to me she could do anything like that.' His eyes gleamed suspiciously bright, as though tears were close. 'I'd pushed it to the back of my mind, until you arrived on my doorstep last week, Imogen.'

Kate's snarl shocked everyone. She sounded inhuman; like a caged animal. 'Julian deserved what he got, and it was all Imogen's fault, not mine.' Her voice rose to a screech. 'I'd invited Julian to the picnic. She'd already taken Greg away from me, and then she got her claws into Julian. It wasn't fair. I couldn't bear it, so I gave Julian a little tap on the head.' Suddenly, shockingly, she sniggered. 'That taught him a lesson.'

Imogen said. 'You got away with murder for thirty years.'

Kate spat back, 'I just wish I'd killed you at the same time, that night. Then, I would have got Greg back.'

The constable tightened his grip on her arm.

Daniel asked, 'But, why the others? The councillor and Greg? Why did you kill them?'

Steph's head jerked up. 'I think I can guess. You and Greg cooked something up, didn't you?'

Kate shrugged. 'We bumped into each other one day when I came back to Somerset to organise a home for my father. My son wanted to see the place I grew up. He went to a football match – Camilton Town were playing Bristol – while Greg and I had dinner at Georgiou's. Greg told me he'd always wanted me, not Imogen, and he'd married her for the rich father-in-law. We made a plan, Greg and I, and I called in to the hotel one evening, to scout out the place.'

Adam nodded. 'You and Greg decided to kill the councillor. His fortune would go to Imogen, and Greg knew she didn't care about money. He planned to get his hands on it all and then you and he would disappear together.'

'Very clever,' Kate's top lip curled. 'It would have worked, as well. It was a good plan.' She gave a little sigh. 'The beauty of it was, no time pressure. We worked on it for months – setting little traps for the councillor's car, draining oil from it, fly-tipping where we knew he'd go. She grinned at Imogen, 'Greg often visited your father. Two of a kind, they were, Greg selling your father goods cheaply off the back of a lorry. No scruples, either of them.' She smiled at her audience. 'I wonder how much of the furniture in the hotel is stolen – passed on from Greg to the councillor at a knock-down price.'

Her laugh grated painfully on Imogen's ears.

'Your father had the luck of the devil. We couldn't kill him, no matter how hard we tried. None of our traps worked. It took so long, we began to think we'd never get our hands on the money, so we had a rethink, and Greg remembered the spiders.'

'Spiders?' Imogen exclaimed, aghast. 'My father hated them – well, he was scared stiff, to be honest – but how did they help you?' And, how could Greg have got involved with this unhinged woman?

'We left a few in your father's car, in the glovebox. Clever, don't you think? I'll admit Greg took care of that part. He wasn't entirely stupid. He bought a load of old scrap from Haselbury House. He'd done some business with the new owner there, got the stuff at a knock-down price, dumped it by the road and threw a few nails on the road itself. Then, he went out and got drunk in Camilton.'

Imogen thought she might be sick. She breathed deeply. She couldn't leave now – she had to hear the full story.

Kate talked on, pleased with her cleverness. 'I phoned the councillor, pretending to be one his latest girlfriends – he always had a couple, the dirty old man, and Greg knew some of their names. I told him the police had called round about some stolen computer equipment and he'd better meet me, or I'd talk. That got him in the car like a shot, and the spiders did the rest.'

Imogen gasped aloud. 'If he saw a spider, he'd panic. He was terrified of them. No wonder he didn't notice the nails on the road.' She thought it through. 'The spiders would have crawled away from the car by the time the vehicle was examined.' It was horribly clever, and her father's worse nightmare.

'Almost the perfect crime, don't you think?' Kate boasted.

Disgust threatened to overwhelm Imogen. 'So, why did you kill Greg?'

Kate's lips twisted. 'He backtracked. He had cold feet. He wanted out of the deal. Said he'd get you back and stay with you.' Hate flashed from her eyes. 'You again, Mrs Wonderful, the oh-so-clever and talented woman everyone loves. You stole Greg away from me, thirty years ago. Then, when I thought he'd come back to me, you stole him again. And I still don't know what he saw in you.'

She spat out the words, venom distorting her face. Imogen shivered.

'I decided Greg had to die, as well. You see, I'd found I was good at killing. Julian's murder was a spur-of-the-moment thing, but his death helped me discover my special talent. It's easy to kill if you're clever enough, brave. Greg's death was a pushover. I did a bit of research on poisons and saw how perfect it would be to incriminate Imogen in her husband's murder. I chose brodifa-coum, because I'd noticed it in the potting shed, that evening I spent with Greg, planning the councillor's death. It was perfect. Wouldn't it have been great to watch Imogen sent to prison?'

Her gaze swept over her spellbound listeners. Her cheeks glowed with delight. 'I bought the poison over the internet and asked Greg to meet me in the orangery, the day of the councillor's funeral, for old times' sake. I dropped a nice big dollop in a bottle of champagne – he loved pinching wine from the hotel – and poured it for him. I kept topping up his glass until his nose began to bleed. He tottered around, panicking, and I ran for it, locking the door behind me with his key.' She sneered, 'Imogen dear, you should put locks on the gate at the back of your precious hotel and sort out the garden keys – Greg stole the spares ages ago . By the way, did you enjoy finding your husband there?'

Imogen watched the woman she'd called her best friend,

horrified at the madness behind Kate's eyes. 'Even then, you hadn't finished. You planted Steph's earring.'

Kate tossed her head. 'Steph dropped it at the reunion and I picked it up. You never know what might be useful. I got my son – our son, Greg's and mine – to take it to Greg's resting place. I told him Greg gave me the earring and I wanted it buried by the orangery, for old times' sake. I gave him a couple of bottles of beer and told him to toast his father after he did it.'

'Oswald found the bottles in the orangery,' Imogen said. 'But, how could you do that to your own son? Involve him in murder?'

Kate grinned and whispered, as though telling a juicy secret. 'Our son's not the brightest star in the firmament, I'm afraid. He takes after his father.'

'Three murders,' Imogen murmured.

'Only three,' Kate confirmed, 'that is, unless you count dogs.' She chortled with glee. 'I hope that big mutt of yours enjoyed the nice juicy steak. I told your manager it was a special treat. I wonder if he's finished it yet.'

Imogen leapt to her feet. 'What have you done? Where is he?'

Before Adam could stop her, she shot from the room, her shriek echoing through the hotel.

'Emily, where's Harley? What did you do with that steak?'

Emily had spent the past hour in the office, pretending not to listen to the drama unfolding in the lounge, but she'd heard every word. She stammered, 'Your friend – that woman in there, I thought she was your friend – she gave it to me in a brown paper bag, when everyone was arriving.'

She sobbed so hard Adam could hardly make out the words.

'It was a present for Harley,' she mumbled. 'She said we were probably too busy with the concert to think about him. I thought she meant to be kind. I was busy, so I gave it to one of the kitchen staff to put in Harley's dish behind the reception desk.'

Imogen ran back into the lounge, waving Harley's bowl. 'He's eaten it already.'

Adam feared the worst. 'Where did he go?'

Imogen rushed to the French doors. 'He must be in the garden. I'll find him.' She ran into the fading evening light.

Adam fought to keep his temper. History was repeating itself – his beloved cat had died at the hands of criminals looking for vengeance. Now, the stray dog who'd lolloped into Adam's heart had suffered the same fate. He pictured Harley lying dead in the grass.

His voice shook with fury as he confronted Kate. He shook his fist in her face, 'You...' he growled. Words failed him.

Kate grinned, red lips curling, showing her teeth. Every trace of the demure, middle-aged facade had disappeared, leaving behind a deranged killer. Excitement dilated her eyes.

Keeping a tight rein on his anger, Adam hissed, 'What did you put on the steak?'

Loving every second of her moment in the spotlight, Kate crowed with triumphant laughter. 'A little treat I bought online,' she exulted. 'It worked so well on Greg; I couldn't bear to let it go to waste.'

'Brodifacoum? Rat poison?'

'Well done, Mr Hennessy,' she sneered. 'You're wasted as a pub owner.' She spun round, hair swinging, and smiled in the police officer's face. 'You can take me to your station now, young man.' She smiled over her shoulder. 'Enjoy the rest of your evening, everyone.'

The old friends left in the lounge sat like statues, too stunned to move.

'What just happened?' Daniel asked.

Adam wasted no time on explanations but sprinted outside, his thoughts whirling. Did rat poison work on dogs? How long would Harley survive? Could a vet save him?

He hurtled towards the orangery, ran up and down beside the stream, but there was no sign of either Imogen or Harley.

In despair, panting with the exertion, he sank onto the wooden bench.

'Harley,' he called, helplessly, squinting into the gloom, 'Where are—' A blow to his chest drove the words from his throat, and sent him tumbling backwards from the bench to the grass.

Harley rested a pair of muddy paws on his evening jacket, breathing gusts of doggy breath in his face.

Adam caressed Harley's ears, muttering nonsense.

Imogen arrived close behind the dog, breathless, as Adam struggled to his feet, brushing grass and sticks from his trousers. 'He's all right,' she gasped, 'at least, I think so.'

'The poison may take a while to work. We need to get him to the vet, fast—'

'No need.' She smiled, white teeth gleaming in the dusk. 'As soon as I found he was safe, I doubled back to the staff entrance and asked in the kitchens. They haven't had time to put the steak in the dish – they said they were too busy.'

Adam let out a shout of laughter, and Imogen joined in.

'Too busy listening to the concert, I suppose. I won't rely on them to feed him in future.'

In the lounge, Imogen's old friends still sat in their circle, talking over each other, trying to understand the extent of Kate's hatred.

They fell silent as Harley appeared, treading mud into the pale carpet.

In the silence, Toni said, 'I never trusted her.'

Steph threw her arms round Imogen.

Daniel's forehead was creased. 'You've got some explaining to do, Mr Hennessy.'

Adam stroked Harley's coat as the dog settled across his feet. To think he'd considered sending this loving creature to a home for strays.

He collected his thoughts. 'As you've heard, your friend Kate hated Imogen for years, ever since your schooldays.'

'But murder – I can hardly believe it,' Steph said. 'We thought Imogen was her best friend.' She shook her head. 'Teenage jealousy is one thing, but murder?'

'Three murders,' Adam pointed out. 'Unfortunately, we don't know exactly what turns a person into a killer. It's a mix of personality traits and circumstances...'

Daniel joined in, speaking slowly, as though thinking through events. 'Kate waited all these years. The hatred must have been like a slow burn inside her, while she did nothing about it.'

Imogen joined in, 'Then, she met Greg again. They rekindled their affair and the hate boiled over into action.'

She shivered. Without a word, Daniel slipped off his jacket and wrapped it round her shoulders.

'Typical Greg,' Daniel said. 'All looks and no brains.'

Adam continued, 'He fought with Imogen, took her savings and left in a huff, but later, he realised he was making a mistake. That was probably his only decent impulse – to beg Imogen to take him back, but, like a fool, he signed his own death warrant; he told Kate his intentions.'

'And she killed him.' Steph's mouth dropped open. 'Just like that. The man she says she loved.'

'What a pair,' Toni said. 'Greg was an untrustworthy idiot, even at school. I bet he was the one who got hold of the LSD for our drinks.' She shivered. 'I didn't realise how lucky I was the day he left me for Kate.'

Imogen said, 'More fool me, for marrying him.' She was carefully avoiding eye contact with Daniel. 'I'm sorry I brought all this on everyone,' she said.

Steph said, 'David, there's one thing that bothers me, but I hardly dare ask.'

David smiled. 'Carry on. Ask me anything.'

Steph said, 'Was there really something between you and Julian? I mean, Kate told me you were a couple and that was why you killed him. We know she was lying now, but—'

David's laugh rang out. 'Were Julian and I a couple? You must be joking. Neither of us felt that way, and Julian only had eyes for Imogen.'

'Like all of us,' Daniel added.

Adam shot him a glance. Daniel had hurt Imogen once. He'd better not do it again.

Steph shook her head. 'Kate said it to keep suspicion away. She must have been worried when we all agreed to meet up, so she set out to muddy the waters.'

'She was an expert at causing confusion,' Adam nodded.

'She fooled us all,' Steph said. 'But, in the end, she was too clever for her own good.'

41

FUTURE

Imogen and Adam strolled through the hotel grounds the next day, Harley bounding back and forth, chasing imaginary rabbits, retrieving enormous sticks and dropping them at Adam's feet.

'He really likes you,' Imogen said. 'Are you sure you don't want him back?'

Adam accepted the dog's latest offering. 'He's much better here with you. He needs space to run. You even have a stream for him to splash around in.' He threw the stick, disappointed to see it fall only a few yards away. 'I need to work on my muscles. Anyway,' he beamed at Imogen over his shoulder, 'have you decided what to do? Will you stay?'

He held his breath, surprised to find how much he wanted her to say yes.

'I never thought I'd say it, but I'm starting to like owning a hotel,' Imogen admitted, and Adam's spirits rose. 'Emily's doing a great job as manager, and I've got used to her now I know she didn't have an affair with either my husband or my father – all she did was work hard. She told me she was terrified when she realised she'd sent my father to his death that day, when Kate rang. We'll build the hotel up again, together.'

'Not giving up the landscape gardening, though?'

'Haselbury House? Not likely. I can't bear to go too long without getting my hands dirty. And when that contract's finished, I can work on the hotel grounds. I have so many plans, I hardly know where to start.'

'Good morning.' Striding over the grass, eyebrows waggling, came Detective Chief Inspector Andrews. 'Glad to see you both up and about, this morning. Whoa—' as Harley charged towards him. 'Nice dog,' he muttered, keeping Harley at bay with one arm.

As Imogen tempted Harley away with a biscuit, Adam said, 'What can we do for you?' He'd never seen Andrews so animated.

'Came to congratulate you. Fine piece of investigation. Very helpful.' That was the nearest to an apology Adam would get for Andrews' earlier attitude. 'Nice work yesterday, too. Good plan.'

Imogen returned alone. Adam raised a questioning eyebrow.

'Harley's with Emily,' she said. 'She's in danger of killing him with kindness. She was in tears again this morning, remembering how close she came to feeding him with poison.'

'Have you forgiven her?'

Imogen considered. 'It shows she's human.'

'I think the two of you will make a great team, and The Streamside Hotel will go from strength to strength. I hope so, for purely selfish reasons. Your success will feed into my turnover in The Plough. Maybe we should try some joint advertising – two great places for food and drink in one village.'

The DCI coughed. 'I thought you'd like to know the mayor confessed to blackmailing your father, Mrs Bishop. Something about stolen plants – couldn't make head nor tail of it, myself. He's going to plead guilty at trial for fraud and corruption over planning permission. There's a string of bribes he wants taken into account, along with his crony, Councillor Smith.' He chuckled. 'Councillor Smith was relieved to get it all off his chest, I suspect. He's more worried about what his wife is going to say.' Andrews gave a hearty laugh. 'I'd like to be a fly on the wall in that house.'

Imogen asked, 'Will people hear about my father? You know, the things he did?'

'Well, it will all come out in court eventually, but I wouldn't worry too much, Mrs Bishop. Receiving dodgy plants thirty years ago won't be big news, and councillors taking kickbacks surprises nobody, these days. Kate Lyncombe's murder trial, on the other hand, will be a huge story – I wouldn't be surprised if it makes the national news.'

'I suppose I can cope with that.' Her voice faltered. 'And Greg?'

'Your husband's crimes were minor, small-time stuff. Not a very talented criminal, I'm afraid. That Joe Georgiou's the one we want. Nasty piece of work, from what we've found so far. We'll be going through his affairs with a fine-toothed comb, I can assure you, working with your old team, Adam.'

So, he was Adam, now, was he? Part of the old police officers' network?

'Seems the man had links with your last case.' Andrews shook his head, as though saddened by the dishonesty in the world. 'I'll keep you informed.' He turned to Imogen. 'As for that silly lie you told…'

She blanched. 'A lie?'

'About your quarrel with your husband. You should have told us the two of you had split up. Police officers weren't born yesterday. My young detective sergeant could tell you were lying; you gave yourself away, blinking and biting your lips. Don't try to pull the wool over police eyes again – you're extremely bad at it. We might have been on to your friend, Kate, sooner, if we'd known your husband had been cheating on you.'

Imogen's face glowed red with mortification. 'Sorry,' she muttered, like a naughty schoolgirl.

'Well, that's what I wanted to say.' The eyebrows twitched again. 'Time to get back to work. Plenty of paperwork for my boys.' He chuckled. 'Told them I want their reports on my desk by tonight. That'll keep 'em busy today. Oh, and there's Constable Stephen Jackson.'

'Toni's son?'

'He's in a spot of trouble – giving information to his mother. Stupid idiot. Still, he's a good enough copper. Not too bright, not up for promotion, but steady enough. He'll get over it.'

He sketched a vague salute and set off back to the hotel.

'Have a good day, both of you. Oh, seems like you have more visitors.' He pointed to a tall figure striding down the path. 'You're popular, today. Let me give you a word of advice. Watch out for that Steph Aldred. Knew her when she was a journalist. Once she had her teeth in a story, she'd never let go.'

Adam laughed. 'If she hadn't suggested the reunion, Imogen and her friends would probably never have met up, and there would have been no justice for Julian.'

Imogen said nothing, her gaze focused on the newcomer.

'Hello, Daniel,' she said.

* * *

Imogen ushered Daniel and Adam back to the hotel. 'Would you like some cake? If the vicar left any on her last visit.' She bustled about the lounge, clattering knives and plates from the sideboard, chattering inanely. 'The best china – we used it for my father's funeral...'

Daniel interrupted, 'I came to get my jacket. I lent it to you...'

'So you did.' She'd forgotten. 'I left it upstairs. I'll get it—'

'No hurry.'

Adam said, 'I'll let you have your sketches back, while you're here. Give me a minute. I'll nip across the road and fetch them.'

Alone with Daniel, Imogen forced a smile. 'How's Steph?'

Daniel stretched out on one of the sofas. 'Fine, I imagine.' He sounded puzzled. 'I haven't seen her, today.'

They didn't live together, then.

A spark of hope ignited in Imogen's chest. She took a breath. This was no time for misunderstandings. There had been far too many already.

She grasped the nettle. 'Are you two an item?'

The slow smile she remembered from the past spread across Daniel's face. 'Not at all. She's a grand woman, of course. We're friends again, after all these years, which is good, but that's all.'

'At the reunion, I thought...' Imogen could think of nothing sensible to say.

He said, 'You and I have thirty years of catching up to do, don't we? How about dinner tonight?'

She made up her mind. No longer an awkward schoolgirl, she would never again waste precious time. 'I'd like that very much.'

ACKNOWLEDGMENTS

Somerset is a well-kept secret. Holidaymakers zip through the country, hurrying down the M5 to Devon or Cornwall. Yet, hidden on either side of the motorway are a multitude of rural treasures: the sandy beaches of Burnham-on-Sea and Brean, the caves of Wookey Hole, Cheddar, where Britain's oldest skeleton was found, and the charmingly named Burrow Mump. What better place for murder mysteries, than Somerset's hidden gems?

I owe a debt to so many people for their help in writing these stories. From the National Trust volunteers who've shown me round Somerset's castles and stately homes, to the vast array of tea rooms and coffee houses where I can sample proper West Country cream teas.

I'm excited to begin this new series of Ham Hill Mysteries, tremendously grateful to the whole team at Boldwood Books for working with me, and especially indebted to my editor, Caroline Ridding, for nursing *A Village Murder* into life, and to Jade Craddock and Rose Fox's eagle eyes. Thank you so much, everyone.

Finally, a big thank you to my fellow members of the

Romantic Novelists' Association chapter in Devon, for their fellowship, understanding and general loveliness, and especially to Jak, an honorary member, for his brilliant ideas.

MORE FROM FRANCES EVESHAM

We hope you enjoyed reading *A Village Murder*. If you did, please leave a review.

If you'd like to gift a copy, this book is also available as an ebook, digital audio download and audiobook CD.

Sign up to become a Frances Evesham VIP and receive a free copy of the Exham-on-Sea Kitchen Cheat Sheet. You will also receive news, competitions and updates on future books:

https://bit.ly/FrancesEveshamSignUp

ALSO BY FRANCES EVESHAM

The Exham-On-Sea Murder Mysteries

Murder at the Lighthouse

Murder on the Levels

Murder on the Tor

Murder at the Cathedral

Murder at the Bridge

Murder at the Castle

Murder at the Gorge

The Ham-Hill Murder Mysteries

A Village Murder

ABOUT THE AUTHOR

Frances Evesham is the author of the hugely successful Exham on Sea mysteries set in her home county of Somerset. Boldwood is republishing the complete series with the next new instalment due in Autumn 2020. Frances is also starting a new cosy crime series set in rural Herefordshire with the first title published in June 2020.

Visit Frances's website: www.francesevesham.com

Follow Frances on social media:

facebook.com/frances.evesham.writer

twitter.com/FrancesEvesham

instagram.com/francesevesham

bookbub.com/authors/frances-evesham

ABOUT BOLDWOOD BOOKS

Boldwood Books is a fiction publishing company seeking out the best stories from around the world.

Find out more at www.boldwoodbooks.com

Sign up to the Book and Tonic newsletter for news, offers and competitions from Boldwood Books!

http://www.bit.ly/bookandtonic

We'd love to hear from you, follow us on social media:

facebook.com/BookandTonic

twitter.com/BoldwoodBooks

instagram.com/BookandTonic

Manufactured by Amazon.ca
Bolton, ON

17858359R00140